# THE BOY WHO PLAYED WITH FIRE

## LIAM MULHALL

*Published in Australia in 2025 by Beacon and Quill Publishing*

*Text copyright © 2025 Liam Mulhall*
*Cover, illustrations © 2025 Liam Mulhall*



Cataloguing Information

A Catalogue-in-Publication entry for this book is available from the National Library of Australia.
A Catalogue-in-Publication entry for this book is available from the National Library of New Zealand.
A Catalogue record for this book is available from the British Library.
United States of America Library of Congress Control Number: 2025916794

*Dewey Number: 813.6*

ISBN (Paperback): 978-1-7641558-2-3
ISBN (Hardcover): 978-1-7641558-8-5
ISBN (eBook): 978-1-7641558-3-0

*Printed in Australia*
*Designed by Liam Mulhall*
10 9 8 7

DEDICATION

To the one who taught me the meaning of love, the quiet inspiration behind Charlotte, and to Oscar, my little mate, whose loyalty has never wavered.

# CHAPTER ONE

## The Boy Under the Table

The pub smelled of old beer and cigarette smoke, the kind of stench that clung to your clothes long after you left. The floor was sticky, the barstools sagged like they'd been carrying the same blokes for decades, and the telly above the bar preached footy like it was gospel. Every pass, every hit, every cheer was delivered like a sermon to the rugby league faithful.

Jax knew the drill. Past the pool table, duck behind the jukebox, and slide under table six. That was his spot. That was his fortress, the place where he could take in the world unseen.

He was six years old, knees tucked in tight to his chest, a battered old Steeden cradled in front of him like it could shield him from everything the world could throw. Outside the table was chaos—men shouting at the screen, schooners clinking, pokies chiming in the corner. But under here? It was quiet. Well, sort of.

Boots thudded around him like soldiers on the

march. Voices barked above him like wild dogs. But the voices weren't angry, only passionate, even obsessed, and it was everything to Jax, cause it was footy.

"Eyes-up footy, that kid's a genius! He sees the play before it even happens!"

"Run a hard line like that and you'll split teams in half!"

"Wrapped him up and folded him in half—textbook tackle!"

The old blokes roared their prophecies, and Jax drank in every word. He didn't just listen, he learned. The rhythm of their voices, the way they tensed before a big play, the knowing silence just before the crowd erupted.

From under the table, he traced shapes in the air— inside balls, cut-out passes, side-steps sharp enough to leave defenders clutching at nothing. He didn't know all the rules yet. He didn't even know every position by name. But he knew movement. Patterns sank into him like muscle memory for a life he hadn't even lived.

If anyone had asked, he knew the basics but could barely explain the difference between a prop and a winger. But he could've told you where the next gap would open, or which bloke was about to get steamrolled. He understood the game the way some kids understood music, not by sheet notes, but by feel.

Jax didn't mind the noise so much. It was silence he dreaded. So, he listened hard, learning not just the words but the pauses, the rhythm, the way men saw the game before the play even started. After a while, he started to see it too.

His dad was at the bar again and he was loud already. Every beer made his voice increase like a volume knob that someone kept cranking up another notch. His mum sat at the edge of it all, still wearing her crumpled nurse's scrubs, the day's weight clinging to her like a second skin. Her smile was thin, not from joy, but something she wore so Jax wouldn't see her falling apart.

She held her drink like it was anchoring her to the room, her eyes locked on a wall that offered no escape, only distance. She was there physically, but her mind was elsewhere. Just a tired heart in a life she never chose, trying to make the best of things for a boy who deserved so much more.

No one noticed Jax under the table. Not when the footy was on anyway. And that was the safest place in the world for him.

The props were giants, hurling themselves into brick walls of bodies with no thought for self-preservation. Kamikaze warriors in footy boots. They smashed forward until cracks appeared. Without them, nothing happened—no metres gained, no space created, no hope at all.

They laid the platform for the rest. The centres, dangerous and elusive, always sniffing around for a half-gap. The wingers, were lightning fast on the edges, waiting to strike given their chance. And in the middle of it all, the halfback, barking orders like a general, hunting gaps where tired defenders tried to hide, counting numbers in the line like algebra on a chalkboard.

The old blokes said he was like a quarterback, only grittier and faster, who didn't mind getting dirty, and willing to take the hit himself. He didn't just pass and kick the ball, he shaped the whole game.

Put it through the hands, sweeping wide, and score in the corner—that was four points. Slot the kick between the uprights, and you had six. The math was simple. The game was anything but. It was the language of victory. Scripture in rugby league.

Then a growl cut through the noise. "Bloody halfback's useless. You watch, he'll butcher this set."

Another voice fired back. "You reckon you could do better?"

"Not now. But back when Troy Mathers still had two good knees maybe he could…"

A third voice joined in, softer, almost respectful. "Troy had more than knees. He could read a backline like a book."

Jax craned his neck and looked above the bar, where a faded Broncos poster clung to the wall, corners curled up and the edges yellowed. In it, a younger Troy Mathers was diving for the corner, Steeden tight under one arm, mouth open with a wide grin. The photo was sun-bleached but still loud enough to tell you he'd been something or maybe even someone once upon a time.

"Could've been anything," the first man muttered. "Until he buggered it all up."

The crowd roared at a try. A schooner slammed

onto Jax's table, making him flinch. Then he smiled to himself in the shadows, holding his ball tighter to his chest.

*One day*, he thought. *One day they'll be yelling my name.*

# CHAPTER TWO

Steel and Bruises

Jax's old man was a man's man, built from steel and silence. Third, in a long line of steelworkers, forged in furnaces and factory yards where worth was measured in calluses and feelings were buried deep. He was big, with broad shoulders, thick arms, and a barrel chest. His beard was coarse and thick, like a steel scrub brush, and his jaw looked like it had been carved from granite. He was a man sculpted by grit, built to endure without complaint. Faded tattoos coiled down his forearms, relics from a youth spent outrunning the shadows of his own upbringing.

He came from Newcastle's rougher side of town, where boys learned to take a hit before they learned to cry. Raised on cold dinners, fists, and short tempers, his father hadn't been gentle, and neither was he. His love came in nods, rough head-pats, and rules barked louder than they needed to be. Jax remembered one night when he came home with a bloodied knee from the playground. His dad barely glanced at it, just muttered, "Walk it off," and turned back to the telly. Not cruel by design, just a man who had never learned softness, trying to make a boy into a man far too soon.

Jax's mum, Melanie, was the softness in the storm, the kind of woman whose very presence made a room feel gentler. Her skin was soft, her hands always warm, and her eyes carried the tired kindness only a mother could wear. She smelled like soap and eucalyptus, and when she hugged you, the world would hush, and your worries seemed to dissipate. A nurse with a heart too big for the life she'd ended up with, she had once dreamed of living by the harbour in Sydney, maybe even wandering the streets of London with a camera and a journal, before such dreams gave way to duty with Jax arrival.

She was the light in a heavy home, always doing her best to keep the peace wherever tension flared. Jax remembered lying in bed after a long day, her tired hands tucking him in, whispering stories about faraway cities. Other nights, she'd hum lullabies, soft and soothing, her fingers scratching lightly through his hair until he drifted off to sleep. Jax loved that more than anything; the sound of her voice, the feel of her touch. It made the world feel okay, even if just for a little while.

But everything imploded the day the steelworks let another hundred men go.

That night his dad came home late. His boots hit the floorboards heavier than usual. He grabbed a beer, collapsed into the chair, and turned the footy up so loud it swallowed the room. He didn't look at Jax. Didn't say a word.

The next morning, he didn't go to work.

By the end of the week, he was gone.

Jax came home from school to find the ute missing from the driveway, the boots gone from beside the door. His mum's eyes were red but she said nothing. The chair sat empty, the telly flickering in the corner like nothing had changed. Jax stood at the front window for days after, waiting for headlights that never came.

No note. No apology. Just silence.

And a boy beginning to understand that sometimes love disappeared without explanation.

At the pub, the old blokes swapped stories about players who could "spot a hole in the line before it opened." Jax would wonder if anyone had ever said that about his father. Maybe he'd played once. Maybe not. But already, Jax had started to watch the game the same way—eyes on the spaces, not just the ball.

He didn't really know the rules. He only knew how the game made him feel — the rush when players broke free, the noise when the crowd roared, the way the bloke in seven seemed to bend everything around him. He shouted louder than Jax's old man ever had, and people listened. The centres gave him a rush, bursting into space so fast it made Jax's chest thump. And the wingers… they flew. Watching them made him believe maybe one day he could too.

Sometimes, that name slipped into the banter, Troy Mathers, just another name in the noise back then, tossed between schooners and arguments over dropped balls. Jax didn't know yet how much it would matter.

By then, Jax was drifting between school and the pub, with nothing much in between. At school, he kept his head down. No one bothered him, and he didn't go looking for trouble, though trouble always seemed to know his address.

His old man had never shown him softness, and it left a mark. There was something in his eyes—a hardness that didn't belong to a boy his age, like he'd already learned that showing weakness was dangerous. It was enough to make even the kids built like brick walls give him a wide berth; word had a way of getting around.

He had a couple of mates, but the pub was where the real lessons came. No bells, no books, no teachers, just the crackle of footy on the telly and the roar of men who carried their lives in schooners and scars. An old bloke once clapped him on the shoulder and said, "Real men play hurt, son." Another told him never to whinge, even when life knocked you flat. Jax listened and stored it away.

It was an education in pride, in strength, in survival. Lessons he would carry long after the scoreboard faded.

# CHAPTER THREE

## The Pub Prophet

The regulars at the pub left him alone while he was a kid, but as he grew up and kept coming round, they started taking notice of him.

"That's Melanie's kid, ain't it?" one of them muttered one afternoon.

"Good lad. Rough hand he's been dealt," another would reply.

They let him stay, bought him a pack of chips, and kept on talking footy like he wasn't even there. But Jax was there. Always listening. Always learning.

From under the table, he started scribbling on stray serviettes, sketching arrows and shapes as the plays unfolded on the telly. He wasn't copying, he was testing ideas—a pass held a fraction longer, a runner cutting in sharper, a hidden offload slipped in traffic. He read the game the way some kids read faces. A slouch in the shoulders, a twitch in a fullback's stance, and Jax knew what was coming. To him, the field didn't run at normal speed. It stretched out, slowed down, every movement carrying a clue if you knew where to look. The old boys clocked it quick.

"Kid's sharp," one of them said, watching Jax mimic a sidestep as he took a bite of a gifted meat pie.

"Got eyes like a hawk," another nodded. "Sees it all. Like he's got built-in slow-mo, I reckon."

It wasn't long before the nickname stuck.

"Oi, Specs!" they'd call out, grinning as he wandered in. "What's the read on tonight's game plan? Up the middle or running shape out the back?"

Jax would smile shyly, offer his quiet answer, then retreat to his usual post with a pink lemonade in hand. Inside, he loved it when they called him "Specs"; it made him feel seen and recognised for something that was special.

The pub was loud and smoky, but he heard things you didn't catch in a classroom. He learned how men spoke when they didn't think little ears were listening, the weight in a silence after bad news, the sting tucked inside a laugh that went on for too long, the way mateship showed up with a hand on the shoulder, a round bought without a word. He listened hard, tucking it all away. Lessons, not from school, but from life.

In the corner near the pokies stood a life-size cardboard cut-out, leaning against the wall like it had been dumped there years ago. Troy Mathers again, this time in full Broncos kit, holding an energy drink with a grin wide enough to sell anything. The colours had faded to pastel, the cardboard warped from the damp, but he could still make out the words printed in bold: "Fuel Your Fire."

Les, a wiry old regular Jax had seen in the same seat every Friday, one of the pub prophets he listened to from under the table, nodded at it, smirking. "Back when he had fire, alright."

Mick, round-bellied and red-faced from too many schooners, was another voice in that same chorus of prophets. He shook his head. "Before the knee. Before Newcastle took a punt on him and he pissed it up the wall."

Jax took another sip of his pink lemonade. Same name as the poster behind the bar, the same story of a bloke who could've been something big, then he wasn't. He wondered how that happened, how did you go from being the one everyone watched to just a cut-out by the pokies, thrown away like an old toy.

The game rolled on, the crowd in the pub groaning when a pass went to ground. Jax's eyes stayed on the number four, the centre. Big but quick, running an inside line before flicking the ball to the winger in one motion. The defence barely had time to react.

"That's how you do it," Les said, slapping the table. "Centre sets it up, winger finishes it. Simple."

*Simple*, Jax thought. But only if you knew how to read it.

# CHAPTER FOUR

One Gone, One Fading

By the time Jax got home that night, the pub chatter still echoed in his head—the slow-mo plays, the way the old boys broke a game down like it was algebra. But the house was different now. Smaller. Colder.

His mum stood by the window, twisting her wedding ring until her finger turned red. She didn't scream or sob. She just sat down and said nothing. No one said the words "gone for good," but kids didn't need words. They knew. Even when you wished they didn't.

In the weeks after Jax's father had left, something shifted in her. Melanie still packed his lunch for a while, still smiled at the school gate. But the sparkle in her eyes, the one that made her feel like sunshine and warmth, had started to flicker.

She stopped picking up extra shifts at the hospital. Then she stopped going altogether. Said she was tired and needed a break, but the break never ended.

The house felt smaller every week, stripped of its warmth. She slept in late, stayed in her robe, and chain-smoked through the afternoons. Dinner was toast or two-minute noodles. Some nights she was jittery, laughing too loud, or scrubbing at the bench until her knuckles reddened. Other nights, she sank into silence, eyes fixed on the television as if it might finally give her answers she didn't know how to ask.

Jax stopped asking questions. He learned to make his own meals. Learned to lock the door at night. Learned to tuck her in when she passed out on the couch. He became the one who held it all together, even if he was just a boy inside, trying to tape up a household that was cracking at every seam.

One night, when the kettle had been whistling for five minutes and his mother didn't flinch, Jax pulled out a notebook a teacher had given him years earlier. He didn't know why, only that his chest felt too full, and the pages felt empty enough to hold it.

He started to write, just words.

*When you're asleep, I talk to you. I tell you the things I'm too scared to say. Like I miss you. Like I still remember how you used to sing in the car.*

It became a ritual. Whenever things got too loud, or too silent, he would write. Little poems, half-thoughts, letters he'd never send. It didn't fix anything, but it helped. The notebook became the only place in the world where he could still be soft, gentle. Where he could still be a boy, even though every other part of his life demanded he act like a man.

And so, the years moved quietly, unevenly, but they moved. His body grew taller, his heart heavier, and his mum kept fading. Yet through it all, he stayed. No matter how broken things were, she was still his mum. And somewhere inside the fog, he still saw the woman who used to sing him lullabies and scratch his scalp until he drifted off to sleep. She was still there, just harder to reach.

So Jax wrote, and waited, and hoped—even if he never said it out loud.

# CHAPTER FIVE

## The Crew

There was Jimmy, the funny one.

Loud, chaotic, and always moving at a hundred miles an hour, Jimmy could talk the leg off a chair, and then apologise to the chair for interrupting. He didn't just walk into rooms, he *arrived*, with a flood of words, bad jokes, and ideas that sounded half-brilliant or half-insane. Teachers either loved him or needed a Valium to survive the afternoon.

Naturally, he had ADD or, as Jimmy called it, "Always Doing Dumb Shit." He once climbed onto the school roof to rescue his drone he'd been flying and accidentally locked the deputy principal in the supply shed. Another time, he planted fake dog poo on the principal's chair and blamed the receptionist. He was the kind of kid who'd paint a mural on the toilet door and get suspended for it, then win an art award two weeks later.

But underneath his mischievous nature was a loyalty

that ran deep. Jimmy could read a room faster than most adults and crack a joke sharp enough to cut through any tension, but he also had this uncanny sixth sense for when someone needed a laugh. He'd take the heat for a mate without blinking. He was either completely zoned in with laser-focused eyes, questions firing like a machine gun, or completely off with the pixies, having a full-blown philosophical debate with a magpie during PE.

There was no middle ground with Jimmy. But his crew didn't need a middle. They needed Jimmy, because Jimmy made the heavy stuff feel light, even if just for a little while. Jax knew about the afternoons Jimmy vanished straight after school, picking up his little sister, making her dinner before their mum's late shift ended. He never complained. Just called it "training for fatherhood."

Then there was Macca, the anchor.

Broad shoulders, thick legs, and built like a fridge. He played front row like it was personal: all heart, no brakes, zero self-preservation. If you saw Macca charging your way, you either braced yourself or moved.

He was always the first to finish his lunch, and probably yours. Once, he downed an entire meat pie in one bite just to prove a point. No one remembered the point, but the legend stuck.

Macca didn't chase the spotlight or attention, nor crack the most jokes. But he showed up when you needed him, whether in rain, hail, or heartbreak. When your world was falling apart, Macca would sit beside you in silence and hand you a sausage roll or anything that was in his backpack of goodies. Those were his love languages: food and company.

Jax also knew at Macca's house there was a lot of noise and very little warmth. Most of the time his family barely noticed if he was gone. Some weekends he'd disappear into his uncle's mechanic shop, elbow-deep in grease, fixing things just to avoid going home. But the boys noticed when he wasn't around, and that made him feel like he mattered.

Then there was Tino, the wildcard.

He was quiet, thin as a rake, and looked like a stiff breeze could carry him away, but his brain was lethal. Tino could solve a Rubik's Cube in under a minute while pretending he wasn't paying attention in physics class. He had theories about everything from footy to strategy to time travel and wasn't afraid to explain them all, even if no one asked.

He wasn't the best with his hands; half the time, he fumbled the ball like it was made of soap, but his boot was absolute magic. He could curl a kick through the uprights from anywhere on the field, on angles that made physics professors scratch their heads. But you never knew which Tino you were going to get on game day, the genius or the gumby. When the genius turned up, it was poetry. The gumby... well, not so much.

And then there was Jax.

He wasn't the biggest kid, nor the funniest, and certainly not the smartest. But he was the one the others looked up to.

Jax had that quiet kind of leadership, the kind you

didn't notice until everything got loud. He didn't bark orders, he didn't need to. One look from him was more than enough to pull a team into line. There was a stillness about him, like a storm just waiting to move. His presence held weight. When he spoke, others listened, and when he didn't, they watched him anyway.

He didn't need to lead by example. He just did it. It was in his nature.

They didn't have a gang name, clubhouse, matching socks, or handshake rituals. They weren't trying to be anything really; they were just misfits. Rough around the edges, a little too loud, a little too fast. But when the world felt too heavy, they carried each other through it.

For a long time, that was everything Jax needed.

They were chaos wrapped in school uniforms, a four-man army of mischief. Jimmy once snuck a live frog into the science lab and introduced it as his "emotional support toad." The teacher screamed, Jax nearly choked from laughing, Macca offered to wrestle it, and Tino named it Trevor and tried to build it a terrarium out of a lunchbox and a paddle pop stick. It was a complete disaster, but the kind of disaster that had them cracking up so hard they nearly fell over — the sort of stuff-up you never lived down.

After school, they always met behind the Andrew Johns Oval. Same busted fence, same graffiti-splashed cricket nets, same unwritten rule that this was their space, away from the rest of the world. Jimmy bounced around with a thousand schemes: "Let's egg old man Cooper's shed!" "Let's build a ramp and launch Macca's bike off the roof!" "Let's put a 'For Sale' sign out the front of old man Jenkins' house again — he lost it last time!"

Sometimes he was too much. Most times, actually. But that was Jimmy, either all-in or off with the pixies. No middle gear. The school counsellor once said, "Jimmy has ADD." Jimmy corrected her without missing a beat: "Nah, I've just got a PhD in bein' a bloody menace."

Macca always brought the snacks. From his own lunchbox, from the servo, from god-knows-where. If there was food, Macca had it. If there wasn't, he was already chewing something mysterious from his pocket. He was the glue of the group. Big, soft-hearted, and impossible to shift, emotionally or physically. He didn't talk much, but you always knew where he stood.

Tino didn't say much either, but he kicked. That's what he did. Always had a half-deflated footy tucked under his arm, and he'd line it up like it was the NRL Grand Final. He'd narrow his eyes, calculate the angle, and launch a drop punt from forty metres out like it was nothing. Pure precision. Pure genius. Jax once asked him how he did it. "Angles," Tino shrugged. "Body weight. Wind direction. Mental projection." "Right," Jax nodded. "So... witchcraft."

They weren't the kind of kids with weekend getaways, perfect families, or new boots every season. But they had each other. And when they were together, even on the worst days life felt a little lighter.

One afternoon, their laughter gave way to

something heavier. They sat on the train tracks behind the abandoned mill, flicking rocks into puddles and half-talking about nothing. The air smelt like rust and eucalyptus. Jimmy broke the silence first. "Reckon we'll still be mates when we're forty?" Macca didn't miss a beat. "You'll be dead before thirty, the way you eat processed meat." Tino added, "If you two idiots are still alive, I'll probably be prime minister!" Jimmy flicked another rock into the puddle, grinning. "Still reckon Specs'll end up with a proper team by then. Kid's too sharp to stay stuck under a table."

They all shook with big belly laughs that echoed down the tracks. Jax didn't say anything. He just stared down at his scuffed shoes, a soft ache blooming in his chest. There was something about that moment — the stillness, the laughter, the knowing — that told him childhood was on borrowed time. They were just four kids with scars under their shirts, laughter in their hearts, and a bond that felt bulletproof. And for a while… that was all that mattered.

# CHAPTER SIX

Warrior in the Garden

Lunch at the state school was chaos in the sun. The oval was split into invisible borders—footy boys in the middle, smokers leaning against the back fence, the handball kings guarding the asphalt courts.

Jimmy, Macca, and Tino were parked on the low brick wall near the courts, halfway through a bag of hot chips Macca had "found" somewhere. Jimmy was mid-story, arms flailing, eyes darting between his mates as he built the drama higher.

"…and then the magpie actually winked at me, I swear on my—"

Four shadows cut across the group. Year Twelve boys, older, broader, with faces already set into hard lines from too many weekends on cheap beer and trouble. The tallest one tilted his head at Jimmy. "Oi, ADHD, battery run flat?"

Jimmy grinned. "Still got enough charge to tell you you're ugly."

The boys chuckled—not kindly. One stepped forward and kicked Jimmy's bag, sending chips skidding across the dirt. "What's the matter, Jimmy? Daddy forget to pack your lunch again?"

"He doesn't have a dad," another muttered, loud enough for them to hear.

Macca's movement shifted but he didn't rise. He was big enough that most knew better than to start with him.

The tallest boy's gaze shifted past them. "Well, look who it is. Your fearless leader."

Jax was walking across the court, shirt untucked and bagging, hanging off to the side. He clocked the scene without breaking stride.

"Oi, Page," the tall one called out. "Heard your mum's a junkie. Loves her little hit more than she loves you, hey?"

Jax stopped. His jaw tightened once. "Say that again."

The boy smirked, leaning forward. "What, that your mum—"

Jax moved before the rest had left his tongue. One stride, shoulder into the chest. His left hand twisted the biggest boy's shirt, his right drove a short, sharp punch into the ribs, then another to the jaw. The tall one hit the ground with a grunt.

Another Year Twelve kid charged him but bounced clean off Macca, who'd stepped in front like a wall. One solid shove from Macca sent the boy stumbling back, swearing as he fell to the ground.

Jimmy was all wild arms, windmilling like he was

trying to swat away flies, while Tino muttered, "Mass times acceleration equals—" before finally stepping forward and firing a shot that clipped someone on the shoulder.

Whistles blew and teachers shouted from across the yard.

"Move," Jax barked, pushing Jimmy toward the court's edge. Macca fell in behind them, like a moving shield. The Year Twelves backed off, muttering and rubbing sore spots.

"Page! To the office! *Now!*" Mr. Harris's voice cracked across the yard.

The principal's office smelled like stale coffee and Old Spice. Jax sat outside on the hard, plastic chair, elbows on his knees, the fight report still fresh in his head.

When he was finally called in, the principal looked up straight away. "Sit down." Jax dropped into the chair, arms folded. "You're a bright kid, Jax. Smarter than most who walk through that door. But you're reckless. Always in the middle of trouble. You've got to settle down because you're running out of chances here." Jax stayed quiet, eyes fixed on a scuff mark on the lino.

"I know life at home isn't easy," the principal said, voice softer now. "But you've got to find another way to deal with things. Because one more stunt like that, and you won't just be suspended, you'll be gone. And I don't want to see that happen."

Jax didn't answer. He didn't need to. They both knew that if the same line was crossed again, he'd do exactly the same thing to protect his mates.

# CHAPTER SEVEN

Nights Like These

It started with a smashed plate. Jax didn't know what had set her off. Maybe the bill on the bench. Maybe the kettle that wouldn't boil as quickly as she wanted. Or maybe it was the ache of a life that never turned out the way it was meant to. His mum had hurled the plate across the kitchen like it had insulted her, like it had mocked how hard she was trying to keep it together. Porcelain shattered against the wall. The shards fell in the sink, then silence filled the air.

She stood there barefoot amidst the wreckage, eyes brimmed red, crying, her chest rising and falling like she'd just sprinted away from something she couldn't outrun. She muttered something he didn't catch, then turned and ran to her room, slamming the door behind her.

Jax had wanted to follow. He wanted to help her, to be the calm in the chaos like he always tried to be. But he knew better by now. He knew that, sometimes, space was the only kindness left to offer.So instead, he grabbed his hoodie, stepped out the back door, and walked.

The air was cold, that heavy kind of cold that went right through you and clung to your bones and made the night feel too wide. Rain started when he was halfway down the street, just a drizzle at first, then thick drops that turned the pavement slick and reflected the streetlights in the puddles.

He didn't know where he was going. He just needed to get away.Away from the house with the broken dishes and TV buzzing with static. Away from the hollow ache that had become his mother. Away from the version of himself that had learned how to disappear just to keep the peace.

He passed the old servo. Passed the empty footy field. Passed a group of older boys smoking under the overpass who muttered something to him, but he didn't acknowledge it and kept on going. His fists coiled in his pockets, knuckles blanched, and his jaw clamped shut like a vice. There were moments he wanted to punch through walls, punch fate, punch every quiet night that left him feeling like a kid pretending to be a man.

Instead, he climbed. A rusted scaffold behind the industrial estate, then an old maintenance ladder, then to the rooftop, flat and silent, overlooking the train tracks and distant city lights. He sat cross-legged, soaked through, and pulled his water-damaged notebook from inside his hoodie.

The pages were warped, but he wrote anyway.

*Rain doesn't ask what hurts. It just falls. Like mums do. Like dads do. Like hope when no one's watching.*

The ink bled in the wetness, but he kept going. Line after line. A silent scream into the paper. Nights like this reminded him of why he wrote, not to be heard, not even to be understood, but to keep afloat. To remember why he was still here.

By the time Jax got home, the kitchen was spotless. No shards, no trace of the storm, except the hollowness in the air. His mum was asleep, her breathing uneven, the kind that came in jagged bursts. Jax lay awake for a while, listening to the rain on the roof, the house settling, and something in himself settling too.

By morning, the weather had cleared. So had his head, just enough to face the day.

# CHAPTER EIGHT

Boys, Ball, and Blisters

Jax was sixteen when he first played rugby league in an actual club competition, where scorelines mattered and two competition points were worth their weight in gold week after week. Up till then, it had only been backyard chaos with Jimmy, Macca, and Tino. But this was different: lined fields, referees, and a small crowd watching, mostly parents and the odd club stalwart. And, to make matters worse, he wasn't even wearing boots. He ran out in battered school shoes, scuffed and too small, held together with three kinds of tape and a prayer. His mates had been playing comps for years. Jax was starting from scratch and was a untaped resource.

No one laughed.Five minutes in, he'd already scored twice, folded a kid twice his size, and thrown a cut-out pass so sharp that a bloke on the sideline spilled his coffee in shock.

It had started, like most things, with his mates.One

afternoon after school, Jimmy had said, "Come have a run with us this weekend."

"Never played," Jax had shrugged. "Not properly."

Macca had bit into his chicken roll. "You talk like a coach. Might as well show us if your boots match your mouth."

"I don't even own boots."

Tino had grinned. "Good. No excuses when you carve up in school shoes."

The field was crooked, the grass patchy. Some kids wore jeans. One bloke had a cricket helmet on "just in case." But when Jax ran out, something clicked. He didn't think of drills or set plays. He read hips, shoulders, eyes, little telltale signs that gave everything away.

They stuck him in the centres, one of the hardest spots to play. You had to be a sprinter, a brick wall, and a chess player all at once—fast enough to beat your opposite, strong enough to stop him, and smart enough to set your winger free when the line cracked. In defence, you had to read the sweeping shapes before they unfolded and shut them down cold.

Their coach, a stocky bloke with a sunburnt face and a gravelly voice, didn't waste words. He just pointed, barked a couple of short instructions, and gave a nod that meant get on with it. Jax had never played under a coach before, and the silence between those few words felt heavier than the words themselves.

Jax didn't know the textbook for any of that, but he knew the pictures. He'd seen them a hundred times under table six at the pub, tracing lines in the air while the old boys called the game.

Their team was chaos. Macca rumbled through the middle like a wrecking ball. Tino nailed a conversion from the sideline, then shanked one from straight in front. Jimmy, sidelined with a rolled ankle, gave play-by-plays like it was State of Origin night — the brutal Queensland vs New South Wales showdown that stops the country: "Page is through the line! Wheels for days, ladies and gents!"

The scoreboard didn't matter to him. The grazes on his knees, bruises on his legs, the mud covering his jersey, the sting of sweat in his eyes, these were what mattered to him. Because for the first time in a long time, Jax didn't feel invisible. He felt *alive*. He felt like he belonged.

As he unlaced his taped-up shoes in the car park, fingers trembling from adrenaline, a man nearby muttered to his mate, "That kid's got a set of wheels."

"Wheels, I tell ya?" the other asked. "Nah. He's got something else. Real footy smarts. You saw the way he read the game? A rare breed they are!" Jax pretended not to hear, and he didn't look over, but the words affected him.

He walked home barefoot that evening, boots in one hand, notebook in the other. Under a flickering streetlight, he paused to scribble a line across a page: *When you've got nothing to lose, you play like it.*

He didn't know it yet, but that muddy field, with only a scattering of locals on the sideline and a tired old scoreboard clicking over, had just become the place where the fire inside him ignited.

And somewhere, not far away, the world had just started whispering his name into existence.

# CHAPTER NINE

## The Man Behind the Fence

Troy Mathers hadn't set foot on a professional rugby league field in over a decade. Not since the night his ACL had gone one way, his ankle the other, and his million-dollar career had snapped like a dry twig under stadium lights with forty thousand fans watching, and one broken-hearted mother crying in the stands. Before that, Troy had been *the* name. *Next Joey*, they said. A freak in the halves. The kid with the golden step and the game IQ that made grown men shake their heads. By twenty, he was on billboards and cereal boxes. By twenty-four, he was on the back of a beer coaster at every pub in Brisbane.

He'd had it all: the speed, the swerve, the swagger. But he also had mates who weren't real mates, habits that held him back, and an ego so heavy it snapped everything that had once been good inside him. When the injury had come, it wasn't just his body that collapsed, but his identity. Rehab followed, then silence, the kind of silence that stung more than pain. No more text messages, no more party invites, no more camera flashes, just a name that mattered only while the jersey was on his back.

Troy tried coaching once, not long after his ACL was healed. The affair lasted two months. He hated the drills, the clipboard, watching younger versions of himself being moulded into something he could never be again. So, he drifted. Worked security, tried media, ran freight; but nothing stuck, nothing sparked his fire anymore.

But something caught his attention that Saturday he stopped behind a rusted fence at a scrubby field in Newcastle and saw a kid in taped-up school shoes tear apart a backline like it was made of paper. The kid wasn't tall, nor was he particularly bulked up, but he moved like he *knew*, like he saw things before they happened.

A sharp step off the left, a perfectly timed fend, textbook tackling that would have left any defensive coach nodding in respect. It wasn't coached, Troy could tell that much from his gut, but had been steadily carved into him from hours of watching footy, absorbing every movement until instinct took over. Jax didn't play like a kid learning the game, he played like a machine built by obsession.

Troy watched in silence, arms folded, hoodie up. He didn't cheer nor clap, he just studied every angle, every touch, every decision.

"The kid reads the line like a fifteen-season vet," he

muttered. Then, turning to the bloke next to him, he asked, "Who's that?"

The man scratched his beard. "Jax Page. Good kid, but full of trouble. Heard his mum's an addict. Dad bailed years ago. Smart-arse too. Never listens."

Troy nodded slowly, eyes still locked on the field. "Yeah… That's what they used to say about me."

That night, he sat in his ute with the window cracked and the notebook on his lap. It had been blank for years. Coaching plans, scouting notes, those had long since lost their meaning to him. But tonight, as he sat with the pen in his hand, he caught himself thinking: talent was raw, but pain made it real. The best players he'd ever seen weren't just tough, they were hurting.

He started showing up more often after that, just watching, quiet and calculated. But something in him stirred, something he hadn't felt since his own playing days: purpose. This wasn't about reliving his past or finding the next version of himself. This was about making sure this one didn't become him.

Troy didn't believe in fate, not anymore. But watching that kid run angry, graceful, fearless, he couldn't help but feel like the game had handed him one last shot. And this time, he wasn't going to drop the ball.

# CHAPTER TEN

Ink Over Noise

The sideline chatter had faded, and the field looked wrecked—grass torn into ribbons, patches of bare dirt shining under the floodlights. Streetlights hummed overhead as Jax made the slow walk home, boots swinging from one hand, the other jammed into his jacket pocket. Mud streaked the backs of his legs like dried blood, and his socks had that stiff, crusted feel from sweat and soil baked together.

After that game — his first real game — Jax caught snatches of voices drifting from the sideline. "He's a natural." "Born for it." "The next big thing." A couple of strangers even clapped him on the back as he walked off, their words spilling over him like they'd just witnessed something special. He nodded politely, but inside all he felt was tired. Not just body-tired. Tired in his soul.

Because he discovered, even in this first game, that with the spotlight came the noise.

Negative talk whirled around in his head on the walk home before the sweat had even dried. None of it stuck, thankfully. What lingered from the spotlight's noise wasn't the cheers, but a heaviness that sank deeper than the bruises—the kind you couldn't see beneath a jersey. The match kept replaying itself in his head. The fend that split the line, the step that left a defender grasping at air; those moments should have been enough. But the missed tackle in the first half, the dropped ball on their own forty, the pass he didn't throw because he second-guessed himself—those pained him more than the hits.

The noise followed Jax down the road, and more was added to it. His mum's blank stare when he'd walked out the door earlier that afternoon, then Jimmy's lopsided grin, Macca's heavy slap on the back, Tino's quiet nod after the game. All of it crowded in his head, but none of it felt like it belonged to him. It was like he was watching from the outside, unsure what any of it meant.

Near full-time, he'd noticed a stranger leaning on the fence. He had his arms folded, a cap pulled low, and he hadn't clapped, shouted, or moved. He just stared at Jax like he was assessing every run and tackle.

Later that night, Jax stood in the bathroom, staring at himself in the mirror. Dirt and grass streaked his neck. Bruises were already rising dark across his shoulders. Mud caked under his nails. His boots dangled by the door, still wrapped in tape. He didn't see a prodigy. He didn't see "the next big thing." He saw a kid who had just survived his first real game, hanging on in water that already felt like it was rising too fast.

The house had gone still by the time he stepped out. His mum was asleep on the couch, the TV muttering through another late-night rerun. The remote dangled from her hand. Jax paused in the hallway, then moved quietly to his room, closing the door against the flicker and laugh track.

He sat at his desk, flicked on the lamp, and pulled his notebook closer. The one place where his head slowed down just enough to hear his heartbeat.

He opened to a blank page. Pen tapping, he finally wrote:

*What if I can't do it again? What if today was just luck? What if I'm not as good as they think?*

The words poured out, raw and messy. Sometimes he imagined someone finding the notebook and reading every page, other times he hoped no one ever would. Because inside those scribbles was the stuff he couldn't say out loud: that even tonight, after everyone was buzzing about his first real game, he felt empty, and the whispers about him being "the next big thing" scared the shit out of him.

He wrote until his hand cramped, until the page was full and the ache in his chest had eased a little. At the bottom, he scrawled one more line, rough, almost angry:

*If fire's in me, let it light the way. Not burn me alive.*

He closed the book gently and slid it under his pillow. The same handful of parents would be on the sideline next week. The boys would hype him up. And the coach would give that short, wordless nod. But for now, in the stillness of his small, messy room, Jax held onto the only thing that made sense.

# CHAPTER ELEVEN

Watching Fire

For Jax, one game turned into another. Saturday after Saturday, he laced up the same battered shoes, ran out on the same crooked fields, and kept proving that his first run wasn't a fluke. He kept playing, and the more he played, the more the whispers grew. Parents leaned on fences, mates ribbed him in the car park, and strangers started showing up just to watch the kid in the centres carve teams open. Once or twice, he even got named Man of the Match. Jimmy never let him forget it, strutting around the car park like he'd won it himself. Jax just shrugged it off, but the words followed him home, louder than he wanted them to.

One of those strangers kept turning up. Jax had noticed him, cap pulled low, arms folded against the rusted fence, but thought nothing of it. Just another bloke watching footy under the floodlights. So, he kept running, kept playing, and tried not to wonder why the man was always there.

Troy Mathers had never intended to stay long. Just a quick look, maybe a couple of sets, then home. But every Thursday night training, and every Saturday game, something kept him there. At first, it was curiosity. A mate had mentioned some kid out west carving up against older boys. But soon it became routine. Without even meaning to, Troy found himself locked in on the same teenager, watching him tear through backlines like he'd been born with a footy in his hands.

Troy could tell the kid hadn't had the academy polish. No one had ironed out his rough edges, no coach drilling him on running clean lines or perfect timing. But there was something in the way he moved, instinctive, raw, and dangerous. A left-foot step planted at the exact moment a defender shifted weight. A fend that snapped a bigger bloke's momentum like a twig. A ball-and-all tackle that dropped a runaway centre dead on the ten.

Troy had spent years around the game. He knew what could be taught and what couldn't. This kid didn't just play footy, he *felt* it. Every pass, every hit-up, every defensive read was the result of muscle memory gained from hours spent watching, studying, soaking it in like his life depended on it.

It wasn't just Jax's step or vision that kept Troy watching. It was the edge in the way he played—every carry loaded with something more than strength, every tackle thrown like it mattered too much. Troy recognised it. He'd played with that same edge once, back when he believed footy might be the thing to save him.

When another Saturday game wound down, Troy stayed in the shadows. The boy walked off laughing with his mates, shoving shoulders, tossing insults, looking alive in a way Troy hadn't felt in years. But later, when the music and banter faded, Troy saw him again. Alone, boots slung over one shoulder, a battered notebook under his arm. His mates blared music and talked about the weekend. Jax walked quiet, steady, like his head was somewhere the noise couldn't reach.

Troy lingered near the sheds one evening, long after most of the boys had gone. Jax stayed behind, packing his gear slowly, methodically. He didn't look up, didn't notice the ex-player watching from the shadows. Troy almost stepped forward, almost spoke. But what would he even say? That he saw himself in the kid? That he knew what it was like to be gifted and grieving at the same time? To have fire in your gut and no idea how to use it without burning everything around you?

He glanced down at his own hand, rough, scarred, the little finger still bent from a game versus Penrith gone wrong, and then back at the boy with busted boots and shoulders too heavy for his age. He didn't see the "next big star." He saw a kid treading water, just barely.

That night, Troy sat in his ute again, window cracked, notebook open on his lap. A single word stuck out. He circled it twice, pressed hard enough to tear the paper: *Jax.*

# CHAPTER TWELVE

## The Four Corners

The day after the latest game, one they'd only just scraped through thanks to Jax's late try in the corner, his body still carried the price. He'd been hammered all afternoon by defenders who had clearly marked him as the one to shut down. Every time the ball came his way, they hit him harder, like he was running with a target on his back. It wasn't adrenaline anymore, just static left buzzing in his legs from the noise he'd been trying to outrun.

He leaned against the brick wall outside the servo, fiddling with a bottle cap, when Jimmy rolled up on his BMX, brakes screaming like a wounded bird.

"What's with the face, mate? Who died? You've been named Man of the Match twice now. You should be struttin' around like a bloody rooster, chest out, feathers flappin'."

"Just tired," Jax said.

Jimmy gave him a squint. "Nah. That's the face of

someone who's been thinking too much. Dangerous stuff for a bloke like you Jax."

Macca arrived next, balancing a pie and a Coke in one hand like he was carrying the crown jewels. He was still in his work polo, dust on his boots, straight from the job site. "Smoko on the run," he said, mouth already full.

Tino trailed behind, earbuds in, mouthing lyrics to a track and clearly not needing anyone else's company. He had his schoolbag slung low, stuffed with books like he was moving house.

They drifted to the park and claimed their cracked concrete bench, their unofficial clubhouse. Jimmy launched straight into a story about a PE teacher who'd tripped over his own whistle cord, complete with squeaks, flailing arms, and a crash landing. Macca laughed so hard Coke sprayed from his nose. Tino didn't join in, he was scribbling in a battered notebook, glancing up at the sky between lines.

"What's that?" Jax asked.

"Equation," Tino said without looking up. "For… forget it. You wouldn't get it."

Jimmy grinned. "Translation: genius crap designed to make us feel like idiots."

"Better than being actually an idiot," Tino shot back, and for a second, even he smiled.

When a group of older boys from his High School called them over for a game of touch footy, Jax and his crew didn't hesitate. It started with casual tags, passes, laughter. But Jimmy's mouth had a way of bending the rules. A couple of "touches" turned into shoulder bumps. Bumps turned into half-tackles.

"Settle down," Macca warned, jogging backwards into position. "This isn't Origin."

Touch footy had its own rhythm, six touches before a turnover, quick play-the-balls and no tackling. But when the older boys tightened the contest, the field started to feel smaller. Jax felt the tension rising. The moment before someone took it too far. The kind of moment he used to run straight into.

This time, he didn't. Instead, he stepped into dummy-half, scooped the ball clean, and spotted a gap where no gap should've been. One step, a feint to the right, then a sidestep left that left two defenders grabbing air. He crossed the chalk and jogged back with a grin he didn't even know he'd started wearing.

"Still got it, Specs!" Jimmy hollered.

By the time the light faded, they were back on the bench, sharing the last of Macca's chips. Jimmy was arguing about who'd actually won. Tino was sketching a diagram of the game in his notebook like it was a crime scene. Macca just leaned back, hands behind his head and eyes half-shut. Jax sat there, legs aching, lungs still warm from the run.

And for the first time all day, the static in his head was gone. Not gone for good, just replaced by the kind of noise you never wanted to block out.

# CHAPTER THIRTEEN

The Proposal

Troy didn't do school visits, he didn't do meetings, and he sure as hell didn't do neckties. But here he was, a few months after first spotting Jax play, sitting in St. Edmund's College as the First Rugby League coach, across from a polished principal in an over-lit office that smelled like lemon wipes and hidden disappointment. The chair beneath him squeaked with every shift, and he tried not to sound like a madman as he leaned forward and said, "I want the kid, Jax Page."

Principal Reid raised an eyebrow, half amused, half wary. "I spoke with the principal from the high school down the road, he said Jax has a disciplinary record longer than a laundry list."

Troy smirked. "The one who sees gaps before they open, drops defenders with a shoulder shimmy, and runs the game like he was born to do it."

"Ah," Reid said, folding his hands on the desk. "That one."

St. Edmund's wasn't exactly a rugby league powerhouse, but it was on the rise. It had invested in decent facilities, had a few rep players, and a coach who once had headlines calling him the future of the NRL. What they didn't have, not yet, anyway, was someone like Jax; raw, electric, and unfiltered.

"He's got issues," Reid said.

"So did I," Troy shot back.

"His mother's unwell—"

"I know."

"His attendance—"

"He'll show up. For footy, he'll show up."

Reid studied him for a long moment, pen tapping lightly against the desk. "You're willing to stake your reputation and your career on this?"

Troy leaned back and crossed his arms. "What reputation and what career? The one I pissed away fifteen years ago?"

It wasn't a yes. But it wasn't a no either.

Troy didn't wait. As soon as he left the office, he marched straight to the payphone near the school gate, jamming coins into the slot with urgency. He called a mate in Welfare space and another contact in the Education Department, anyone who could help grease the wheels and push the right paperwork through. The real challenge ahead had little to do with eligibility forms and signatures, and everything to do with trust and timing.

That afternoon, he drove to Jax's house. The letterbox was stuffed full of swollen bills, takeaway flyers, and crumpled fast-food coupons spilling out like no one had cared for weeks. The front gate groaned as he pushed it open, the paint flaking off in his hand. A broken mug sat on the step beside a single shoe, which yearned for its mate to return. He stepped onto the porch, each board creaking under his weight. The floor was splintered, the screen door hanging off one hinge like it had given up years ago. Troy knocked once, then again. Nothing. On the third knock, he stepped back and glanced through the grimy window.

Inside, Jax's mum was slumped on the couch, a cigarette burning low between her fingers. A mountain of dishes was piled up in the sink behind her. The television hissed with static in the background. The whole house felt like it had been put on pause, like life had pressed stop and forgotten to press play again.

Troy didn't say a word, he turned around and walked back to his car, sat behind the wheel, and stared blankly through the windscreen.

He'd seen talent before, and plenty of it. But he'd never seen fire like this, not just in the feet, but behind the eyes. And he knew, deep in his gut, that if someone didn't reach out soon, that fire was going to burn the whole damn place down.

"You get one chance to change a kid's life," he muttered to himself. "Don't waste it."

# CHAPTER FOURTEEN

When Opportunity Knocks

Jax sat cross-legged on his mattress, his journal open in front of him. A blunt pencil rolled across the page, stopping in the crease. Half a sentence sat there, scratched out mid-thought. The words weren't flowing in his head tonight, only fragments, images, and feelings he couldn't quite name.

He sighed and leaned back against the wall, rubbing his face. He heard a low rumbling from outside, the growl of the engine and the brakes squealing, a sharp sound against the still night.

Jax eased to the window, parting the curtain just enough to see without being seen. A bloke in a dark hoodie stepped out of a battered ute and shut the door with a deliberate thud. He was tall and broad-shouldered. His stride was slow but certain, the kind that said he owned whatever ground he walked on.

At first, Jax figured he'd never laid eyes on him, just another stranger. But then something snagged, a shard of memory. The way the bloke's head dipped before scanning the street, eyes sharp and unhurried. The faint swagger in his step, like he'd walked this ground before. Jax's chest tightened. He couldn't place the face, but the feeling was there, familiar, like a memory just out of reach. The man knocked the door to Jax's house once. Waited. Then he knocked another time. Still no answer. On the third knock, he stepped back, glanced toward the dirty lounge room window, then shook his head and walked back to the ute. Jax watched as the truck pulled away, taillights disappearing down the street. He didn't think much of it at the time, but the bloke's face got lodged somewhere in his memory, like a splinter.

The next afternoon at training, he saw him again.

The sun hammered down, the hard-packed field behind the servo throwing heat back through Jax's boots. The boys were loose, tossing cheeky offloads, trash-talking about who'd carved up most on the weekend. Jax half-listened until his eyes caught a flicker of movement near the fence. A figure stood there, hood shadowing his face, motionless, as though the noise and chaos of the game could never touch him. That watchful stare was familiar, Jax knew it was the same bloke. Jax tried to look past him, but after the session wrapped and the boys peeled off in pairs, the man stepped forward. "Jax Page?" he asked.

Jax turned, eyes narrowing. "Yeah… who's asking?"

"I've been trying to find you," the man said. "Came by your place yesterday."

"That was you?" The man nodded. Jax shifted his

weight, folding his arms. "Am I in trouble or something? What've I done now?"

A small chuckle. "Nah, you're not in trouble, mate. Far from it."

Jax didn't move. "So, what's this about then?"

"I'm Troy Mathers. I coach the First Rugby League team at St. Edmund's College."

Jax raised an eyebrow. "The private school?"

"That's the one."

"And what, you scout kids out the back of servos now?"

Troy smirked. "Only the ones who've got more to them than they let on."Jax stayed silent, but the line burned a little too close to home. Troy's tone shifted, losing the banter. "Look... I've seen talent before. You've got something else, kid. If you don't learn to harness it, it'll burn you from the inside out. I know, I've been there before."

Jax's guard slipped, just a fraction.

"I'm not here to sell you a dream kid," Troy said. "I'm offering you a shot. A place at St. Edmund's, full scholarship. New kit, new boots, a new school. None of that's the real point. What matters is making sure a kid like you gets the support he's earned. I can see it in you, and I'm not about to watch it waste away." He pulled out a card and held it out. Jax hesitated before taking it.

"Talk to your mum," Troy said, stepping back. "Have a think about it." Then he turned and walked away, leaving Jax standing in the heat, card in hand, unsure if the whole thing was real or just some weird dream.

That night, Jax lay on his back in his bed, the card on the pillow beside him. His phone glowed in his face as he searched "Troy Mathers rugby league."

Dozens of articles came up. *Golden Boy's Career Snapped in One Tackle. Teen Prodigy Falls Short of Greatness. ACL Injury Ends NRL Dream for Broncos Halfback.*

He clicked on one, a photo of Troy as a teenager, grinning beside a cereal box with his own face on it. Another headline caught his eye: *Newcastle Knights Offer Redemption Deal to Fallen Star.*

He read on. Troy Mathers signed a one-year deal with the Knights on the back of his ACL injury after the Brisbane Broncos parted ways with him, but the fairytale didn't last long. He missed training, missed rehab, turned up to training half-cut. Another wasted shot.

There were photos, too; Troy slumped outside a pub, a mugshot where he had bloodshot eyes, split lip, and a hollowed expression. And then one more, Troy in a St. Edmund's polo, speaking at a lectern. The caption read: *Ex-NRL Halfback Finds Redemption in Coaching.*

Jax let the phone drop to his chest and stared at the ceiling. This bloke had reached the pinnacle and lost it, he had crashed harder than most would ever know. And now here he was, offering Jax a way out.

Maybe he wasn't full of it after all. Maybe he saw Jax not just for what he could be, but for who he already was.

# CHAPTER FIFTEEN

## The Offer

The card sat on the kitchen table the next day, its gold crest glinting under the sunlight, black edges too sharp for a house full of soft, fraying things. His mum was sitting on the lounge, same as always, half watching the TV, half off in another world. A cigarette was burning down in the ashtray, another already lit between her fingers. The curtains were drawn even though it was still daylight outside. The house felt like it was holding its breath, while outside, the world moved on without them.

Jax hovered in the kitchen doorway before crossing to her. "Mum," he said softly.

She turned her head slow, hazy. "Yes, Son?"

He sat across from her, elbows on his knees. "Did you see the card on the kitchen table? The school one?"

She nodded, eyes narrowing a fraction. "St. Edmund's, wasn't it?"

"A coach came to see me yesterday. His name is

Troy Mathers. He… he offered me a scholarship. At St. Edmund's. A full ride with new gear, proper training facilities, better schooling, everything."

Her lips parted but no words came straight away. She just looked at him, really looked, like she was trying to see something in his face she'd forgotten years ago. "Is that what you want?" she asked finally.

"I think so. I don't know. Feels… big. Like I'm dreaming it."

"You're not dreaming, Son," she said quietly. "And it sounds like you've already made up your mind."

He glanced at his hands. "I just don't want you thinking I'm leaving you behind."

She let out a dry laugh, not mocking, just worn, like someone who'd used up all her big emotions long ago. "Jaxy, if someone's offering you a way out of here, even just a sliver, you take it. Grab it with both hands, and run."

"You reckon?" he said, chewing at the inside of his cheek, torn between excitement and the weight of leaving her behind.

"I know so. You were never built for small places, Son. Not with that heart, that fire. And maybe now, someone else sees it too."

They sat in the quiet, the TV humming under something bigger. Then, he stood, started for the hallway, but her voice stopped him, soft and worn. "You'll still come home though, yeah?"

He turned halfway back. Smoke curled around her like old memories. "Always," he said. "Love you, Mum,

LUB14." She gave a small nod, like that was all she needed to hear.

He didn't tell the boys straight away.

How did you explain to your best mates that you're leaving the school where you used to punch on behind the bins, skipping class to sit on the oval talking shit about girls and footy? How did you look them in the eyes and say someone's pulling you out of the only world you've ever known to wear a tie and sit in a classroom full of kids whose lives have been mapped since birth?

It wasn't just any offer, it was a full ride. New school, new boots, and a shot at something more.

He knew they'd crack jokes, rip into him about his blazer and silver spoons. That's just how boys were. But a small part of him was scared. Scared they wouldn't get it, that they'd think he was leaving them behind.

# CHAPTER SIXTEEN

New Colours, Old Ties

The scholarship came through faster than Jax expected, faster than anyone could have. One day he was lacing up his boots on the patchy grass field behind the servo, and the next, he was holding an official letter with the St. Edmund's College crest stamped across the top.

The servo was busy when he finally decided to tell his mates. Cars pulled in and out, the hot stink of fuel clinging to the late-afternoon air. Jimmy was perched on the milk crate out front, BMX tipped against the wall. Macca leaned on the bin with a sausage roll in one hand, Coke in the other. Tino stood on the curb, earbuds in, tapping his foot to something.

"Boys," Jax said cautiously between bites of his chicken roll. "I've got something to tell you."

That got their attention. Jimmy slid off the crate, leaving his bike propped against the wall. Macca shoved the last of the sausage roll into his mouth, wiping his hands on his pants and followed. Tino tugged one earbud out and eyes fixated on Jax now.

Together they drifted over to their usual cracked concrete bench, their unofficial clubhouse. Jax leaned forward, elbows on his knees.

"So… I might be switching schools," he said.

Jimmy froze mid-chew. "You say what now?"

"St. Edmund's. Full scholarship."

Tino's eyebrows rose. "Deadset?"

"Yeah. The coach came out, watched me play, and made the offer."

For a second, silence. Then Macca broke into a grin. "You? In a blazer? Mate, I'm framing that photo and its going straight to the pool room."

Jimmy jabbed a finger at Jax's boots. "Think they'll give you ones that don't need half a roll of tape to stay together?" They all cracked up, the kind of laughter that's part pride, part shock, part awkwardness.

Tino nudged him. "You gonna take it?"

Jax looked down at the battered boots. "Yeah," he said, quiet, but sure. "Yeah, I am."

Jimmy reached over and snatched the rest of Jax's chicken roll. "Then you better get used to sharing with the private school kids. Starting now."

"Oi!" Jax barked, grabbing at it to get it back.

Underneath the banter, the nerves shifted. They weren't gone, only edged aside for now. Beneath the digs and jokes, he knew what they were really saying was: "We're proud of you, mate."

Behind the scenes, Troy was working the phones and knocking on doors to smooth Jax's move to St. Edmund's. He even rang the principal at Jax's state school to get a straight rundown.

The principal didn't sugarcoat it."Page? He's a handful. Bright, but a drifter. Always in fights. Never hands in homework. Good kid underneath it all, but reckless."

Troy barely blinked. "Sounds like someone I used to coach," he said.

He promised to be responsible for Jax. Told them he'd mentor him directly, watch his grades, keep him focused. He believed not just in Jax's ability, but in the kid himself. He saw potential, but more than that, he saw a young version of himself still clawing for air, desperately seeking a way out.

As the first day at St. Edmund's approached, word started spreading. It's what happened in towns like Newcastle, footy towns, blue-collar, rust-belt, heart-on-your-sleeve towns. People knew when something's brewing. The whispers started at the servo, in the barbershop, at the corner pub over schooners and Sunday footy.

"You heard about that Page kid? Got a full scholarship."

"St. Edmund's? No way. That's a long step up from dustbowl footy!"

"Kid's got wheels and hits like a truck, too. Reckon they're targeting him for rep."

The streets were talking. Coaches were listening. Scouts were lurking. Jax, though, he was still just a kid trying to figure out how to tie a bloody tie.

# CHAPTER SEVENTEEN

The Private School

The morning of Jax's first day in St. Edmund's College, the boys walked Jax to the front gates. The school looked like something off a postcard: towering, sandstone buildings, manicured hedges, and perfect lawns. It had gold-painted crests above the archways, and gates so tall they looked like they belonged to a castle, not a school. Jax stood there for a moment, taking it in, his new uniform hanging awkwardly on his frame, pants a bit too long, collar stiff and tight. He tugged at it like it was choking him.

Jimmy whistled. "Mate, you look like a politician's bodyguard."

"Nah," Macca grinned, "he looks like he's about to argue someone's tax return."

"Shut up," Jax muttered, but he smirked. Their voices were familiar, loud, and loose. A welcome reminder of home.

Tino nudged him. "Hey, try not to get eaten alive in there, Mr. Scholarship."

"Yeah," Jimmy added mock-seriously. "If they try and make you join the debate team, blink twice and we'll come save you."

They all laughed, and Jax laughed too, the kind of laugh that stuck in his chest as they gave him quick back slaps and wandered off towards their state school down the hill. Then it was just him. Alone.

The first thing Jax noticed about St. Edmund's wasn't the buildings, it was the silence. No yelling, no swearing, no footies bouncing off classroom walls, only well-behaved kids in polished shoes, whispering behind blazer sleeves. He stepped through the gates and felt like the whole place was holding its breath.

Word travelled fast in Newy. The new kid from the west side, on a footy scholarship, known for his hits and his home life. The footy boys noticed him quick. He got a few nods here or there, and one or two even smirked at him.

One kid, clean-cut, private-school polished, leaned to a mate and muttered, "That's the one with the junkie mum, right?" Jax heard it. He stared straight at him and didn't say a word—he didn't need to. The look from Jax shut the kid up cold.

Training that afternoon was brutal. Coach Troy gave him nothing. "You want to run with this squad, Page? Earn it." So, he did. He ran like he was chasing something no one else could see, tackled like he was wrestling ghosts, and played like the game was the only thing keeping him alive.

By the end, his knuckles were bleeding, scraped raw;

his shirt was soaked through, and his eyes burned as sweat ran down his face. But no one could deny it: Jax was a freak.

In the change rooms, the silence returned. There was no banter, just as tension filled the air. Jax knew that game, the outsider tax, and he wasn't willing to pay it. He dried off, packed his gear methodically as usual, and left without a word.

Later that night, he sat on the edge of his bed. His mum was asleep down the hall, still sober, for now. The fridge was full thanks to the food voucher Coach Troy had slipped into his bag at training without saying a word.

Jax opened his notebook and wrote: *I don't fit here, and I don't fit there either. Maybe I'm like a boot without laces, it still works but never sits right.*

Then, he closed it, leaned back, and stared at the ceiling, thinking about all the trials still to come.

And for the first time in a long time, he let himself wonder: *What if I actually belong somewhere?*

# CHAPTER EIGHTEEN

## The First Hit-Up

The whistle blew and, for a heartbeat, everything stopped. Jax felt that familiar tunnel vision, the eerie stillness that settled in just before first contact. The opposition stood across the field in navy and gold, looking polished and powerful, like a well-built machine. They were bigger, cleaner, sharper, the kind of team that expected to win before the ball was even kicked. St. Edmund's had been losing to them for years. But this year, they had Jax.

Jax sat on the bench, mouthguard tucked in tight in his sock, jaw clenched, eyes locked on the game. Coach Troy had benched him deliberately, not as punishment, but rather as a statement. At this school, respect wasn't handed to you, even if you were already whispered about being the next big thing. You had to earn it.

The first ten minutes were an unbridled disaster. St. Edmund's dropped the opening kick-off, gave away a penalty, and leaked a try through their right edge that made the parents groan with disbelief. The assistant coach leaned in and muttered quietly, "Get Page on now."

Troy didn't even blink. He gave one quick nod and told Jax to "Go fix it."

Jax got up from the bench, wide-eyed and ready for battle, then slipped his mouthguard in, gave Troy a slight wink, and jogged onto the field. Most of the boys barely acknowledging him, except one, Matt Easton, the tall, clean-cut, team captain. The same smug voice who'd whispered about Jax's mum in week one.

He clapped slowly, and said with sarcasm thick in his tone, "Let's see if the new messiah can save us now, lads." Jax didn't bite, he didn't need to. He'd let the boots do the talking.

His first touch came off a quick tap from a penalty, no time for a set play, no blockers running decoys, just raw instinct. He charged at the defensive line, timing his run to hit the gap between the front-rower and the second-rower. One tackler got folded on contact, another clung to his jersey for dear life and then got dragged three meters before being shaken off like a ragdoll. The impact of the hit echoed across the field. The sideline roared, some gasped.

But Jax didn't react. He got up calmly, played the ball fast to keep the momentum going, and turned and got set back in the line for more.

Two sets later, St. Edmund's worked a short side play off the ruck. The halfback stabbed a grubber kick along the ground towards the try-line behind some tired defenders. Jax sprinted after it, diving low to regather the ball picking it up and placing it down in the in-goal to score a try. He still did not celebrate, just wiped the blood from his lip quickly before jogging back to halfway.

St. Edmund's clawed out an eighteen to fourteen win, their first against this team in years. After the game, the boys huddled in the middle, sweat-soaked and stunned. Matt Easton finally looked at Jax and gave a short nod. "Nice hit-up," he said

Jax didn't smile. "Next time, pass me the ball," he said, already walking off.

In the sheds, the air began to shift. A quiet comment here, a laugh there. Tension gave way to banter. And then, from outside the sheds, a familiar, booming voice echoed across the yard: "Oi, Big League! You finished being famous yet?" It was Macca. Jax couldn't help it; a grin broke across his face, just for a second.

Back home, his mum was sitting on the front step waiting for him, sober and awake. "Heard you scored," she said.

Jax shrugged. "Ball just landed in the right spot, I guess."

She snorted. "Bullshit." She handed him a lukewarm meat pie. "You're going to be someone, Jax. I know it."

He didn't reply, just looked out at the street, the weight of her words settling into his chest. Something had stirred deep in him.

Respect couldn't be bought nor begged for, but today, with one hit-up, he'd started to earn it. And, for the first time he could remember, he let himself believe that maybe he could be something.

# CHAPTER NINETEEN

Recess Wars

Jimmy was halfway through a meat pie when the bell rang for second break. He looked around the courtyard of St. Edmund's with a smirk, pastry flakes clinging to his jumper.

"So, this is where the rich kids eat," he said, chewing noisily. "Bit sterile, ain't it?"

Jax shook his head, already regretting this. "You're not even supposed to be here."

Jimmy flashed a grin. "Mate, we were born to be here. Cultural exchange, you know?"

Behind him, Macca lugged a backpack the size of a toddler, overflowing with snacks, while Tino followed at a safe distance, muttering about how this was a blatant breach of school visitor policy.

Coach Troy had tried to set it up as a quiet, casual drop-in to bring a little of Jax's old world into the new one and help him adjust. The plan had lasted three minutes. By the time they'd reached the quadrangle,

Jimmy had already challenged a Year Ten to a thumb war, Macca was double-fisting chip packets, and Tino was mid-interrogation with a confused student about the school's rugby league GPS tracker system.

A prefect approached Jimmy, unimpressed. "Do you even go here?"

Jimmy didn't miss a beat. "Do you even understand the socio-economic inequality of this postcode?" he replied, biting into a custard tart he definitely hadn't paid for.

Jax stood nearby, arms folded, half-amused. All week he'd felt invisible, drifting between classes like a ghost, whispered about, judged without a word. But now, with his boys here, loud and chaotic as ever, it was like he'd become visible again. Not necessarily understood but seen.

Matt Easton watched from a distance with a few of his mates, arms crossed. "Friends of yours, Page?"

"More like family, Easton," Jax said.

Easton snorted. "The short one just tried to sell me a packet of chewing gum."

"That's him networking," Jax shrugged.

But it wasn't long before things went sideways. Jimmy, riding a wave of confidence, snatched a soccer ball from a group of Year Nines and hoofed it across the quadrangle. The ball arced high and slammed into a teacher's coffee cup, sending a spray of liquid across the courtyard.

Then there was silence enough to hear a pin drop.

Jimmy froze. "Might've… misjudged the wind there, I reckon."

Ten minutes later, the four of them sat in the principal's office. Jax lounged, arms crossed. Jimmy was quietly building a tower out of sugar packets. Macca was halfway through a stolen chicken burger. Tino launched into a calm, detailed explanation of how the coffee incident was "technically an accident and, more importantly, a demonstration of Newtonian physics."

Coach Troy rubbed his face and sighed. "They're not *bad* kids," he said.

Principal Reid raised a brow. "They're *your* kids, then?"

Troy glanced at Jax, then at the others, sugar towers, chip crumbs, nervous rambles and all. "Yeah," he said. "They are."

On the way out of the Principle Reids office, Jax pulled Jimmy aside. "You know you're a menace, right?"

Jimmy grinned. "Yeah. But I'm your menace."

For the first time in weeks, Jax laughed. A proper one from his belly, not just his mouth. They didn't belong here, not really. But together, they made sense. And for Jax, that was enough to keep showing up.

From across the courtyard, Jax spotted a girl watching. She was pretty, the kind of polished, put-together pretty that stood out in a place like this. Dark hair tucked neat, blazer sharp, notebook resting on her lap. Even from a distance, there was something structured about her, like she belonged to a different world than his.

She didn't look away when the boys in blazers stared, or when the teachers' lips tightened at him and his mates cutting through the quad. Her eyes stayed on him, steady and unreadable. Jax couldn't tell if she was unimpressed, curious, or both. But she didn't flinch. Not once.

When the bell rang, she snapped her notebook shut and slid it into her bag. Jax didn't know her name yet, but something told him he'd find out soon.

# CHAPTER TWENTY

Charlotte

Charlotte Walton had noticed the new boy before she ever sat beside him. Yesterday in the quadrangle he'd been flanked by three mates who looked like they'd been dropped into St. Edmund's straight from another planet, loud, grinning, and unapologetic. They'd turned break time into a spectacle, but somehow, he had looked like the calmest one in the middle of it all. He hadn't flinched when people stared. He hadn't apologised. He hadn't tried to fit in. And that was what stuck with her.

Now he was at the front of Science Block B, waiting as Mr. Clarke read out seating allocations. "Charlotte Walton, you'll be with… Jax Page."

She blinked once, offered a smile that might've doubled as a wince, and looked him over as he slouched toward her desk. His shoes were scuffed, his uniform crumpled, and a fading bruise lingered under his right eye. He didn't look scared of anyone—if anything, he looked bored, like nothing here was worth his time.

Charlotte sat bolt upright, her open notebook already divided neatly into headings and subpoints, highlighter uncapped next to it. She was the sort of student teachers trusted with the whiteboard markers—organised, punctual, the kind who colour-coded assignments for fun. Her hair was tucked neatly behind both ears, and her pen clicked three times before she started writing, always.

Jax dropped into the chair beside her and leaned back like he owned the place. Charlotte didn't move, didn't let herself react. She annotated; he doodled skulls in the margins. They were opposites sharing the same lab bench, and the distance between them was loud.

Ten minutes passed before she finally spoke, eyes fixed on her work. "Do you even know what biochemistry is?"

He tilted his head toward her. "Is that like… cooking with a lab coat?"

Her exhale came sharp and short through her nose. "Right. This is going to be fun." She kept writing, letting the silence hang. "Why are you even here?" she asked eventually.

"Because they kicked me out of Hogwarts."

Charlotte didn't look up. "I'm being serious."

"Seriously? I'm here because I'm good at running into people really hard and not dying."

She set her pen down, finally meeting his eyes. The bruise, the slouch, the way he delivered the line without even trying for a laugh—none of it made sense. "Well, I'm not doing all the work."

"Didn't ask you to," he said easily.

"Didn't say you had a choice," she shot back.

That was the start of it—a flicker of tension that held her attention in a way she hadn't expected. He didn't squirm, didn't apologise, didn't even smirk. He just sat there, steady under her gaze. And that was what unsettled her most of all.

Charlotte wasn't sure what she saw in him yet. Not a project, not a prodigy. A puzzle, maybe, one she didn't have time to solve, but one she couldn't stop noticing.

# CHAPTER TWENTY-ONE

## Netball and Nuisance

PE was a joke, or at least, that's how Jax saw it. Even at a private school, the PE bibs were dodgy, stretched out, sweat-stained, and carrying a smell that no wash had ever fixed. Worse still, he'd been paired with Charlotte again.

"Mixed netball," Mr. Carmody had announced like it was a gift. "Great for agility, communication, and spatial awareness. And yes, boys, it's a non-contact sport, so keep your testosterone in your pockets."

Jax rolled his eyes. He was used to training with intent where bruises were earned, lungs burned, and drills had a purpose, but here he was, running around a polished indoor court in non-marking shoes, chasing a ball he wasn't even allowed to hold for more than three seconds. It felt more like a physio warm-up than sport.

Charlotte, Miss Straight Spine and Sharper Tongue, stood beside him, hair tied so tight it looked like it hurt. She scanned the court like she was planning a military exercise. "Just don't do anything dumb," she said without looking at him.

Jax smirked. "Define dumb." She didn't bite.

The whistle blew. Jax kept it simple at first, with chest passes, quick cuts, and easy give-and-go plays. But instincts died hard. A loose ball rolled toward the sideline, and he chased it down, scooped it up in one fluid motion, and without thinking, fired a bullet pass across the court.

Charlotte snatched it mid-flight, steady hands absorbing the sting. "Jesus," she snapped. "This isn't rugby league."

Jax cracked a grin. "Do I look like a meathead?"

"Yes," she replied flatly.

He laughed, genuine this time. "Sorry. Force of habit."

She shook her head but didn't hide the tiny upward twitch at the corner of her mouth. For a moment, it almost felt... easy. Two players learning each other's game. She was quick and precise, while he was unpredictable and instinctive. It worked better than either of them admitted.

By the end of the lesson, Jax was flushed and winded, but smiling. It'd been a long time since he'd enjoyed a class. As they packed up, Charlotte handed him a worksheet with his name already filled in at the top.

"I figured you wouldn't do it," she said.

He raised an eyebrow. "And you did it for me out of... pity?"

"Let's call it insurance. You flunk, I get dragged

down too." She said it like a contract, no sympathy in her voice, just terms and conditions. Jax stared at her, worksheet in hand, wondering how someone could be so infuriating and yet so intriguing.

The school loudspeaker crackled. "Mr. Jax Page, please report to the Rugby League office."

Charlotte raised a brow. "What did you do now?"

He half-smiled. "Might be a rocket, might be a reward."

Coach Troy's office looked like it had survived a paper cyclone, full of scribbled whiteboards, game plans, magnets scattered like chess pieces mid-match, and a training jersey draped over a chair like it had collapsed there after a loss.

"Shut the door," Troy said without looking up. Jax obeyed. "You've been here, what? Six weeks?"

"Something like that."

"You're making waves," Troy said. "On the field, obviously. But I'm hearing things from staff, too." Jax stayed quiet. "I'm not here to grill you. I just want you to get one thing, this scholarship isn't a free ride. Keep your head screwed on. In class, around school, and around town. It all counts."

"I know."

Troy finally looked at him. "You've got talent, Jax. Real talent. But I've seen boys like you before. Hard kids, brilliant on the paddock, but gone before they're eighteen. I'm not watching that happen again."

Jax looked at the floor. "I'm not like them."

Troy leaned forward. "You're strong, sure. But

you're carrying more than most, and if you don't learn how to handle it, it'll crush you." He let the words hang a moment, then his tone shifted, quieter. "How's your mum?"

"She's alright."

"You sure? You guys need anything? Food? Help?"

"We're good."

Troy studied him for a moment, then pulled an envelope from his desk. It was thick, with folded hundred-dollar notes inside. He slid it across without fanfare.

"No one needs to know. Call it a scholarship bonus. It stays between us. And you're starting in the centres this week."

Jax nodded, slipping the envelope into his bag quickly, careful not to let anyone see. It felt heavier than money—belief and trust pressed into every fold.

Later, when he stepped into the late-afternoon sun, shadows stretched long across the oval. He pulled his mouthguard from his sock, turning it over in his hand, thoughts racing. This wasn't about waiting on benches or hiding in the background anymore. Troy believed in him—not just the player, but the person.

For the first time in a long while, Jax didn't feel like a misfit stitching himself together. He felt like he belonged. He felt like a teammate.

A kid with a shot, a chance to change his stars.

# CHAPTER TWENTY-TWO

## The Coach's Office

Troy Mathers sat alone in his office long after the bell had rung. The footy jersey hung off the chair like a tired body after the final whistle, reeking faintly of old sweat and winter grass that had clung to it for years. The whiteboard looked like the aftermath of a battlefield, with arrows carved into it in haste, magnets scattered like fallen soldiers, names scrawled in thick, black marker—Page, Morrison, Leota—each one carrying the weight of the game, and also, of their own story. His coffee was stone cold, same as yesterday, same as most days, but he still took a sip out of the cup anyway.

The door had barely clicked shut behind Jax when Troy leaned back, eyes on the empty hallway. He pictured the tall frame, the silent nod, the boy slipping that envelope into his bag like contraband. Carrying more than just money, carrying the weight of all of it.

Troy leaned back, closed his eyes, and for a moment

he wasn't forty-three anymore. He was eighteen, his boots in a training bag, fingers still taped from last weekend's trial, that same raw fire burning in his chest. Back then, everyone said he had it, the step, the fend, the fight. And for a while, they were right.

There were girls, fast cars, and even faster nights. Money in boot deals before he'd earned them. Signing bonuses that had mates suddenly circling like flies at a barbecue wanting to be in his corner. Then one bad landing, that trademark step, a pop, a scream, and his ACL was gone. With it went the career he'd wrapped his whole identity around, a career torn before it had even properly began.

What had buckled wasn't just his knee, it was him, his identity. Then had come the silence, when the calls stopped. Then, the pills to dull the ache, and then, he turned to drinking and gambling to drown the noise. The drugs came later to carve out a brief escape from a world gone dark. But the hardest blow was to his pride, that hollow, bone-deep knowing that he'd been the one who could've made it.

He pushed those past memories away, like they were smoke, to the back of his mind, and opened his eyes up. Jax's name stared back at him from the list. There was something in that kid. Something more than just fend, strength, or fast feet. He played with fury, but also with purpose, like he wasn't just trying to win, he was trying to be seen. Troy knew that look. He'd worn it once, too.

But it wasn't the on-field stuff that worried Troy most. It was what he saw in between. Jax trying to hide the bruises, the tired eyes behind his quiet stares, the way his shoulders stayed tight even in warm-up drills.

Troy had seen a hundred versions of kids like him on a footy field, hard, hungry, and gifted. Most didn't fail because they lacked skill or talent, they failed because no one taught them how to carry the baggage they couldn't leave at home.

Not this time.

He'd already bent the rules, he had peeled cash from his own drawer and slipped it across the desk without a ceremony. Told himself it was nothing. But he knew exactly what it was. It was a lifeline.

He stared at his empty mug, then at the chaos on his desk—training notes, schedules, plays scattered everywhere. With a sigh, he stacked the papers into one neat pile, if only to stop the clutter closing in. Balance, he thought. The one thing harder to coach than footy.

The kid needed drills, but he also needed structure, support, a village, a tribe. And maybe, just maybe, Troy still had enough left in the tank to be that for him.

He stood, cracked his neck, and looked out at the oval one last time before locking up. Jax Page wasn't going to slip through his fingers. Not on his watch, and not this time!

# CHAPTER TWENTY-THREE

My Mum's Not Dead

Charlotte hadn't planned on trailing Jax. She only meant to call out when she saw him slip off school grounds without a bag or a hall pass. But by the time she opened her mouth, he was already half a block ahead, moving with that same grim purpose, like he had somewhere to be and no time to waste. She hesitated, then quickened her pace. It wasn't curiosity that pulled her after him, not really. It was the way his shoulders sagged, the weight in his stride—too familiar, too much like her brother the morning he'd never come home.

She kept her distance, far enough back to pretend she wasn't following, close enough to see when he turned down quieter streets lined with weathered fences. After only a couple of blocks, he entered a tired-looking house with a sagging step and a bin left too long on the curb. Charlotte slowed on the footpath, questioning why she'd even come this far.

Then it came: the shriek of a kettle, then silence, and then a crash.

Her body moved before her thoughts caught up. She hurried up the steps and knocked. No answer. She tried again. This time the door creaked open, just a crack.

Jax filled the gap. Shirt untucked, chest rising too fast, eyes flicking like he was working out which version of himself to let her see.

"What are you doing here?" His tone balanced uneasily between annoyance and surprise.

"I… saw you leave. Just wanted to check you were okay," she said.

The air that slipped through the gap hit her first— stale and heavy, carrying the sour tang of old takeout, cigarette smoke, and something damp beneath it all. She couldn't see much past him, just the dim light and shadows, but it was enough to know this house didn't feel like a home.

Jax shifted, and for an instant she saw the lounge. His mum was on the couch, half curled, barely conscious, her eyes glazed and fluttering. Her face was pale, hands twitching slightly. A shattered mug lay in pieces on the floor.

Charlotte froze, but Jax was already moving. He glanced back once, voice low. "Stay there."

He stepped inside, crouched, and began gathering the shards like he'd done it a hundred times before. Charlotte stayed in the doorway, her hands hovering uselessly, unsure what to do.

"You can say it," Jax muttered. "She's a mess. I'm a screw-up. I should be in class."

Charlotte swallowed. "I wasn't going to."

"She's not dead," he added quietly. "In case you were wondering."

"I wasn't," Charlotte said. "I just… didn't know."

After that, the room sank into silence. Jax lowered himself to the floor, cross-legged in front of the coffee table, staring at it like it might give him answers. Charlotte drifted back against the doorframe, leaning into it for support. The only sound was the low hum of the fridge, filling the space they couldn't.

"This is why I didn't finish the science sheet," Jax murmured. "Some days, I'm too busy making sure she's still breathing."

Charlotte didn't know what to say. So, she crossed the room quietly and sat beside him on the floor. She didn't speak. She just stayed there, steady and present.

After a while, Jax stood, grabbed a spiral notebook from the bench, and shoved it under a pile of unopened letters. Charlotte noticed, but she didn't comment.

In those moments, she saw him more clearly than she ever had before. Not the boy who joked in class or threw bullet passes in PE. Not the "scholarship kid" everyone whispered about. Just a son worn thin, carrying more than he should, holding up the roof with bruised hands and no instruction manual.

"My mum's not dead," he'd said. But in some ways, she was. And Charlotte, more than she'd ever care to admit, knew exactly what that felt like.

# CHAPTER TWENTY-FOUR

## Ghosts We Don't Talk About

Charlotte didn't speak a word about what happened that day. Not to her friends, not to her mum, not even to herself, really. She just tucked it somewhere behind her ribs, the way Jax had looked, sitting on the floor like it was the only solid thing left in his life. She couldn't unsee it; the quiet, the weight, the way he'd cleaned up the broken mug like it was his normal daily routine.

She knew that kind of quiet. Her brother Eli had it, too.

He had been older than her by seven years. Strong, athletic, full of swagger when he wanted to be. Everyone thought he was bulletproof, the kind of boy who could carry the world on his shoulders and still smile while doing it. But even strong boys crack eventually, especially when their dads disappear without saying goodbye.

Charlotte had been ten when their father left. Too young to fully understand, but not too young to notice the change in Eli. He didn't say much, just got quieter, moodier, and angrier, like he'd swallowed something heavy and never found a way to spit it out. And maybe that was the part she didn't get until later, the way a father's absence on a boy doesn't just leave a space, but also a question: "What's wrong with me?"

Eli never said it out loud, but she heard it anyway, in the way he quit showing up to footy practice, in the way his laughter slowly faded away. In the way his fists came up quicker than his smile. She used to think he was just being a teenage jerk, but now, she knew better.

Sometimes, boys don't fall apart all at once. Sometimes it's a slow burn, quiet, an invisible burden they feel they need to carry. And by the time anyone notices, it's already too late.

After Eli died, people told her it wasn't her fault, that you couldn't always see it coming. But she had seen it, not clearly, not in words, but in the silence. In the way he had stopped asking for help, and in the way no one had offered it.

So now, years later, when Jax walked out of school with that same quiet slouch, she felt it in her chest like déjà vu. That night, Charlotte lay in bed, staring at the ceiling. Her mind went back to the way Jax had said, "She's not dead… in case you were wondering." She understood more than he could possibly know.

Because Eli's body had died, but the boy she'd loved, the one who snuck her chocolate and called her "Squirt," had been gone long before. Sometimes death didn't come with sirens, sometimes it started quietly, when no one's watching.

Charlotte didn't know what to do with all of this. She didn't want to fix Jax, he didn't need saving. But maybe, just maybe, he needed someone to see through the noise, someone who didn't flinch, who didn't look away. And maybe, though she couldn't quite admit it yet, he was doing the same for her.

They were both carrying ghosts. These ghosts bore different shapes and different names, but ghosts from the past they remained. And, for the first time in a long time, Charlotte didn't feel like she was carrying her weight alone.

# CHAPTER TWENTY-FIVE

## The Chemistry Test

Jax didn't like tests, rows of desks, the way the fluorescent lights buzzed overhead like a warning siren. He didn't like how Charlotte sat bolt upright, pencil sharpened like a bayonet, ready to wage academic war.

"Multiple choice and a short answer," Charlotte announced.

"Cool," Jax said. "I choose option D, none of the above." She didn't laugh, not even a smirk.

They'd been paired again, randomly or so the teacher said. Charlotte probably thought the teacher was trying to fix him, but Jax figured the bloke just enjoyed torturing her.

"You measure, I mix?" she offered, snapping on gloves with the precision of a surgeon.

"You mean like a team?" he replied.

"I mean like damage control," she said, already lining up the beakers.

Jax didn't bother reading the instructions, he didn't need to; he watched Charlotte's hands instead. Every movement was precise, measured, and deliberate. "You're good at this," he said.

"Because I read, Jax."

"I read too. Usually signs that say, 'Do Not Enter.'" Still nothing, like a stone wall.

But then, as they began heating a beaker of hydrochloric acid to react with magnesium strips, Jax said casually, "You know, it reacts faster if you warm the acid first. Higher temperature means more kinetic energy, more collisions, and a faster reaction."

Charlotte blinked. "How do you know that?"

He shrugged. "I don't know. I just remember stuff."

"From where?"

"Science class. Maybe. Or TikTok." He smirked.

She stared at him a moment longer than usual, a glint sparking in her eyes. "You're not as dumb as you act, are you, Mr. Page?"

He gave a half-shrug. "Depends who's watching."

As they packed up, Charlotte handed him a folded-up practice quiz. "Here. Just... keep it between us, okay?" she said.

He took it from her. She passed it over like it was nothing, but it wasn't. "What if I fail?" he asked.

"Then you try again," she said. "That's how people learn, Page."

He looked at her, really looked. Not in a crush way, not yet, just... curious. "You always talk like a school captain?"

"You always pretend like you're not scared?" she shot back, but then her eyes flickered, just for a second, like she'd remembered something she didn't want to. She closed her bag quickly. "I've gotta go." Before he could answer, she was already halfway out the door.

That night, Jax sat at the kitchen table with the quiz open and a pencil in hand. His mum was asleep again and the house was quiet. He flipped to a blank page in his personal notebook and wrote: *She sees through me, and she doesn't even flinch.*

Maybe he didn't need to impress her. Maybe just showing up was enough. And maybe Jax was smarter than he'd ever admitted, just waiting for someone to believe it.

# CHAPTER TWENTY-SIX

## Fries and Footy

The scene hit him first; their old stomping ground, the local burger joint opposite their state school. Hot oil, salty chips, that familiar smell that clung to the air and your clothes like something dead or dying. Mr. Wong, the owner, was still behind the counter, same apron, same stooped shoulders, same quiet nod of recognition as Jax entered. He used to always throw in an extra dim sim. Maybe he felt sorry for Jax. Maybe he just thought the kid needed fattening up. Either way, Jax had always appreciated it. A wave of nostalgia crept over Jax, unbidden, as if the room itself had reached back and pulled him into old memories.

Jax spotted the boys in the far corner, already posted up at their usual table, burger wrappers spread like battle trophies and chip boxes almost demolished. Macca was mid-story, arms windmilling as he recreated his under-eights grand final try for the hundredth time, that sidestep that beat the fullback, the dive over the line to score the try, and the pretend roar of the crowd.

"There he is!" Jimmy called, grinning. "Mr. Private School himself. Come bless us with your shiny shoes and big words, bro." Jax slid into the booth, grinning, and swiped a handful of chips from Tino's tray before he could protest.

"I swear," Macca said, pointing at him, "you smell like a library and rich-kid shampoo."

"Do they even eat carbs there?" Tino added. "Or is it all protein shakes and tofu salads?"

Jax smirked. "Nah, today's lunch was character development and humility. Two servings of it."

Jimmy snorted. "Big man's learning jokes now. Next thing you know he'll be correcting our grammar."

They cracked up, and for a moment it was like nothing had changed, like things were before scholarships, before the weight of expectations, before life got so bloody complicated.

"You miss it?" Macca asked, jerking his chin toward his old state school across the street.

Jax shrugged. "Yeah… sometimes."

"What's it like?" Jimmy asked. "The new joint?"

Jax leaned back. "Polished. Everyone knows which fork to use at dinner and how to spell 'entrepreneur.'"

"Do *you* know how to spell 'entrepreneur?'" Tino asked.

"Not the point," Jax shot back.

Macca's eyes narrowed. "And the footy?"

"Starting centre," Jax said. "Coach reckons I've got vision."

Jimmy grinned. "Course you do. You've been watching footy since you were six years old, drawing plays on napkins, calling yourself 'Specs.'"

"That was the old boys at the pub," Jax corrected. "Name just stuck."

Jimmy smirked. "Speaking of sticking… Charlotte, aye? Can't open Insta without seeing you two in the same frame."

Jax groaned. "Here we go."

"You've been mentioned, brother. Chemistry class, PE, footy training, she's following you around like a bad smell," Jimmy teased.

"She's either tutoring you or flirting," Tino said, grinning.

"She's… different," Jax admitted, quieter now. The table went dead quiet which was rare for this crew.

"You like her?" Jimmy asked.

"I don't know," Jax said truthfully.

Macca leaned in, eyes wide. "Bro, that's either love or a superpower."

Jimmy tossed a few more chips at him. "Don't overthink it, Specs. Just don't screw it up."

Jax stared at the chips in his hand, then popped them into his mouth. "Not planning on it."

They all nodded like it was settled, the way boys did when feelings ran too close to the surface and food filled the gaps.

Outside, streetlights flickered on, bathing the street

in an amber glow. Inside, the laughter rolled on, the digs got sharper, and the debate shifted to whether the Broncos' new fullback was worth all the hype, with at least three different versions of what "worth it" meant. For Jax, it was exactly what he needed; grounding, a reminder of where he'd come from.

He didn't know what tomorrow would throw at him. But tonight? It was fries and footy. And that was all he needed.

# CHAPTER TWENTY-SEVEN

## Recess Replays

After fries, banter, and the comfort of old mates, the silence of Monday hit harder than usual. Things were different now. Jax had a locker, a timetable, a group chat he still hadn't replied to. His name was scribbled on the noticeboard next to "Man of the Match" from a game they weren't even tipped to win. And at recess, a few of the footy boys actually sat near him. Not next to him, not yet, but close enough to notice he was there.

Even Matt Easton gave him a reluctant nod, like it pained him to admit it. "Good read on that edge play," he muttered after a gym session.

"Didn't want you getting beaten on your outside again," Jax replied.

In rugby league, the "edge" was where teams would use attackers to swing wide with various plays. It was the strip of turf between the middle of the field and the sideline. Read it wrong, and the other team tore you apart. Read it right, and you shut them down.

Matt cracked a grin. "Appreciate that."

What lay between them wasn't friendship, yet the battle lines had faded, leaving a fragile truce.

Most days, Jax still ate alone. But today, as he peeled open a cold and flattened meat pie from the bottom of his bag, a familiar voice piped up behind him. "That thing used to be food, or…?" Charlotte, hair tied back, chemistry textbook under one arm, smirk locked and loaded.

"Breakfast of champions," Jax said. "Want some?"

"No, I value my internal organs," she shot back, and then plopped down onto the bench beside him without asking.

They talked about nothing for a bit: footy, science, why the canteen food always smelled like wet cardboard. At one point, Charlotte nodded toward the notebook poking out of Jax's bag. "Didn't peg you as a writer, Page."

Jax froze. "I'm not," he said. "I'm just a bloke who needs somewhere to put the shit he can't say out loud." She nodded once and didn't push the point.

Just then, someone walked past, someone from the old school. Darren. Same year, same crew once upon a time. Now he was dressed in the same blazer and tie as everyone else, though his collar was crooked and his headphones still hung around his neck. He paused, eyes locking onto Jax's.

"Private school now, huh?" he said, loud enough to

sting. Jax stiffened. "Who are you pretending to be, Page? One of us?" The words landed like a stray boot to Jax's ribs. Darren smirked and kept walking, laughing under his breath.

Charlotte glanced sideways. "Friend of yours?"

"Used to be," Jax muttered, eyes on the pie he no longer felt like eating. He didn't say much after that, and neither did Charlotte. When the bell rang, she stood and looked down at him.

"You don't have to prove anything, Jax. Not to them, not to anyone." He didn't answer, because he wasn't sure he believed her.

That night, he wrote: *The past has claws. It grabs me when I'm not looking. One minute I feel like I'm climbing, and the next, I'm slipping again.*

Fitting in had never been the goal, and belonging, that was even harder; that took time. Belief, that took everything.

# CHAPTER TWENTY-EIGHT

Bleeding with a Pen

Jax handed her the notebook after class, slipping it across the desk while everyone else rustled bags and scraped chairs. He didn't say a word. Charlotte blinked and took it carefully, as if it might break in her hands. "What is this?" she asked.

"You'll see," he said.

She expected it to be a joke, a doodle, maybe something about footy drills, or his rugby league dream team. What she didn't expect were pages upon pages of heartfelt pain. That night, she sat on her bed, knees drawn up, the hum of her bedroom fan soft in the background as it circled above and read it. Slowly, carefully, page after page of barely legible scrawl.

It had no structure, no rhyme, just feeling, lines that didn't try to be perfect, they just told the truth. *I talk to the ceiling when the silence gets too loud. Mum said sorry once, but I don't think it was to me. Every time someone leaves, I feel less worthy, and it makes it hard wanting to stay.* She didn't cry nor pity him, but she did press her fingers to her chest when she read one line over and over: *Sometimes I write to stop myself from disappearing.* It hit different, because she knew what it meant to disappear, even when you were right there in the room.

The next day, she slid the notebook back across his desk without a word. No scribbled message, no explanation—just the weight of her eyes holding his for a moment longer than usual. In that silence, something changed. What had been respect was now trust, and that trust edged into something deeper, quieter than a crush but stronger than simple flirtation.

After class, she followed him outside. The air was warm, the world noisy, but around them, everything felt still.

"You're a good writer, you know," she said.

"Nah," he replied. "I'm just bleeding with a pen."

"It still counts," she said. She paused, then added a little softer, "You ever think about showing someone else?"

"What, like a publisher?" he said.

"No," she replied. "Just someone who might need to see it."

Jax didn't answer, he couldn't, because the truth was he already had.

That night, he opened the notebook again. The same one he almost never let anyone see. He turned to a page she'd dog-eared, her quiet way of saying *this mattered.* Beneath the last line, he wrote: *She read my mind and didn't run.* Then he tore that page out, folded it, and tucked it into the side pocket of his schoolbag, where he usually kept his mouthguard. He didn't know why yet, only that it felt right, like something was beginning. It wasn't love, but it was safety and intimacy, and for Jax, that was rarer than gold.

# CHAPTER TWENTY-NINE

## Like Fire and Water

Charlotte was the only one who'd ever really seen him. But that didn't mean Jax wanted to stay seen. The next week, he was different, quieter, withdrawn. Like someone who'd given too much away and now needed to pull it all back. Charlotte caught him at the school gate one morning and asked, "You okay?"

He just shrugged and muttered, "Yeah. Just tired." But he wasn't, not in the physical sense, anyway. He was tired of feeling open. Tired of the weight that came after letting someone in.

At lunch, she brought up his writing again. "That stuff you wrote, you ever show it to your mum?"

He flinched, not obviously but enough for her to notice. "Nah," he said. "She's got enough on her plate."

But Charlotte didn't back down. "Maybe it would help her, knowing how you feel."

Jax stared at the table. "She's not the one who needs help," Jax said, voice low. The words landed between them like bricks, heavier than he meant them to. He wasn't talking about his mum, not really. He meant himself.

Charlotte didn't flinch. She just held his gaze, steady and unafraid, like she could handle the weight of him, even when he didn't want to carry it himself.

Charlotte thought about pushing, about telling him people didn't just fix themselves, that waiting until it's too late was the worst kind of mistake. But the memory of another boy who use to close his bedroom door stopped her cold. She'd been here before, standing in the exact same place, trying to save someone who didn't want to be saved, and the ending still lived under her skin and echoed in her memory.

She picked at her sandwich, eyes fixed on nothing. When she finally spoke, she said, "You make it sound like letting someone in is a weakness, Jax."

"Depends who you let in," he said.

The conversation hung there, unfinished. She let it drop, not because she didn't care, but because caring too much had once blown her world apart.

That night, Jax walked the streets with his hoodie up, hands in his pockets, the notebook burning a hole through his backpack. He drifted without thinking until he ended up at the oval. It was empty under the hum of the floodlights. He dropped his bag, pulled out a footy, and started running drills, alone. Step, spin, hit the line. Again, and again, and again. It was his therapy, his way of saying "I'm still here."

When he got home, his mum was asleep on the

couch, peaceful for once. He grabbed a blanket and tucked it around her gently before heading to the kitchen. Sitting under the dim light, he pulled the notebook from his bag and flipped to a blank page. His pencil hovered before he scrawled: *She wants to understand me, but what if there's nothing good to find?* Then another line: *I'm not scared of Charlotte. I'm scared of what she'll do with the truth.* He closed the notebook and stared at the cover.

Fire and water, that's what they were; he burned, she cooled. And somehow, they balanced. But balance was delicate, and storms were already building.

Sometimes the hardest thing wasn't letting someone in. It's keeping them there when both of you were carrying ghosts from the past.

# CHAPTER THIRTY

Storm Season

By the time Jax got to school on Monday, the whispers had already started, but they were not even about him; they were about Charlotte.

"Heard she's been hanging out with him."

"Did you see them at the shops?"

"Why would someone like her be with *him*?"

It was the kind of schoolyard poison that didn't need a firm basis of truth from which to spread, just attention. And attention was the last thing Jax wanted.

Charlotte shrugged it off like it didn't bother her, but Jax could tell she was faking it. Her eyes lingered longer than usual on her books, her laugh had a forced edge, and she didn't sit with him at lunch.

"I'm just not in the mood," she said when he asked. She didn't look up when she said it, just kept tracing the edge of her book with her thumb. For a second, something flickered in her face, the kind of shadow you got when an old memory cut across the present. She recovered fast, but Jax caught it. He didn't know what it was, only that it wasn't about him.

He nodded and didn't push, though inside, he felt the rumble building.

Then came the maths class incident. One of the boys, a slick-haired AFL type — the polished, too-cool-for-school kind — named Aiden, leaned across to Charlotte and said, just loud enough for the class to hear, "Didn't think you were into charity cases."

Half the students laughed. Jax saw red. He rose slowly, every inch of movement heavy with threat. His desk screeched across the floor, the sound sharp enough to cut through the noise. Chairs shifted, other desks scraped back as kids pulled away, and one by one, the laughter died. Heads turned. Eyes fixed on him.

"Say that again," Jax said.

"Touchy, are we?" Aiden smirked. "Didn't realise your leash stretched this far."

Jax slammed his hands under the desk and heaved, flipping it over. The legs screeched across the lino before it crashed onto its side.

Jax's knuckles blanched, veins standing out against skin pulled tight, fists still clenched around nothing. His chest heaved, shoulders coiled, every muscle straining like he'd just lifted the whole room with his bare hands.

Before it got worse, Mr. Halston, the maths teacher, stepped in. Jax got detention for two weeks.

Jax didn't care about the punishment. He cared that Charlotte hadn't looked at him since. He cared that the demons he kept caged had slipped through the bars. And most of all, he cared that the mask he had tried so hard to hold steady was slipping. He wasn't just fighting them anymore, he was also fighting the version of himself they believed in. The angry kid, the lost cause, the fire that consumed everything around it.

That night, Jimmy messaged him: *Heard what happened in class today mate—Aiden's a dick. You all good?* Word must've flown through the St. Eddie's boys fast; Jimmy had been across their names and stories for weeks now, even from another school.

Jax stared at the screen, didn't reply, then set the phone down and walked to the back shed. He grabbed his notebook, opened to a blank page, and wrote: *It's storm season. Inside and out. And I don't have an umbrella.*

Some storms started with words, others began with silence.

# CHAPTER THIRTY-ONE

Charlotte's Story

They sat in the bleachers after training, sweat still glistening on their skin, the stadium lights humming quietly above them. The rest of the boys had trickled off, but Jax stayed, because Charlotte had stayed. Not long ago, she'd been keeping her distance, ducking out of conversations, finding excuses to slip away. But lately, something had softened. She didn't look through him anymore. She stayed. And Jax had come to realise that her presence was the one thing that calmed the fire inside him.

Charlotte sat with her knees pulled up, arms hugging them tight, eyes distant. "I haven't told many people," she said, her voice barely above a whisper. Jax turned slightly to face her, sensing this was something important, something real. "My brother… he took his own life."

The words landed like a stone between them. They felt heavy, real, finite. Jax blinked. "Charlotte, I… I didn't know."

"Hardly anyone does," she said. "People talk about him like he disappeared, but he didn't. He was here, and then he wasn't."

She paused, drawing in a shaky breath. "He was funny. Like, annoyingly funny. Always quoting movies, always making everyone laugh. But inside, he was hurting. A fake smile hides a broken soul, you know.?"

Jax nodded slowly. He knew that feeling. The mask, the silence, the battles no one saw.

"I used to think if I'd just said the right thing," she continued, "maybe he'd still be here."

"Charlotte…" Jax reached over, placing his hand gently on hers. "You can't carry that."

"I know," she said. "But it's hard not to."

Silence wrapped around them again. But this time, it wasn't awkward. It was sacred.

"You remind me of him sometimes," she admitted. "Not because you guys are the same, but because you carry weight in your eyes and in your heart. Like you've seen things most people haven't. And you still get up. You still care."

Jax swallowed the lump rising in his throat.

"I think that's why I… why I wanted to get to know you better." She looked up then; she looked vulnerable and brave. Jax didn't say anything right away. He didn't need to. He just held her hand tighter.

For the first time, he saw her, all of her. Not just the smart girl in class, the one who challenged him, but the one who had been through her own fire and survived. In that moment, something deepened between them.

What settled between them wasn't love, but a deeper recognition—an understanding, a connection that needed no words, only the truth of being seen.

And, for now, it felt like his heart was quiet for a moment.

# CHAPTER THIRTY-TWO

## The Letter

He found it by accident. It was tucked between the pages of his journal, behind old assignments, crumpled drawings, and unfinished lyrics. His quiet place, his confessional, the only corner of his life that felt untouched by other people's hands.

No one else knew about it, no one else was supposed to. That's why the corner of a folded piece of paper jutting out where it didn't belong made him freeze. His fingers hovered over it before pulling it free. The paper was light but felt heavy in his hands.

Charlotte's handwriting, small and careful, the kind of neat that didn't happen by accident, like she'd written it more than once, pausing, crossing things out, starting again until it was exactly what she wanted.Jax sat on the edge of his bed. The house was quiet except for the ticking of the old hallway clock and the distant hum of the TV his mum had left on. He unfolded the note slowly, almost scared of what it might say, or what it might mean.

*Jax,*

*I wasn't sure if I should give this to you, but I think you've gone long enough without knowing what people really see when they look at you.*

*You act untouchable, like nothing gets through, but I've seen you when no one else is watching. You carry too much—your mum, your mates, your past—like no one else could take the weight.*

*Even strong backs break. You don't always have to be the fire, you don't always have to be the one holding everyone else up. Sometimes, it's okay to let someone see what's underneath. The kid who writes those poems, the boy who gets quiet when the noise gets too loud, the boy behind the fire.*

*I'm proud of you, and I get it more than you think. You're not the only one who's learned to smile when it burns. Even if you can't see it yet, I do.*

*— Charlotte*

Jax didn't move. The letter hung in his hands like it might vanish if he blinked. He read it once, again, then a third time, slower. No one had ever put him into words before, not like this.

That line, "the boy behind the fire," stayed with him, sparking in the quiet. She'd reached through every layer he'd built, the scowl, the mouthguard in his sock, the armour he wore without thinking, and found the part he kept locked away. And she hadn't flinched.

The bit about "smiling when it burns" stuck too. He didn't know what she'd been through, not really, but there was a weight in those words that didn't come from guessing.

He folded the letter carefully and slid it back into the journal. Not hidden this time, just resting there, where it could remind him on the days when his chest felt like stone that someone had seen the real him and stayed anyway.

For the first time in a long time, it didn't feel like he was carrying it all alone. He let the mask slip, just a little. And for tonight, that was everything.

# CHAPTER THIRTY-THREE

## Blood and Thunder

It happened after school. Jimmy was walking past the bus stop near Charlestown Square, hoodie half-up, earphones in, hands in his pockets, when he heard them behind him.

"Oi. Weirdo." Three of them wearing blazers from Newcastle Grammar, the rival school with posh ties, polished boots, and a reputation for arrogance.

Jimmy turned, pulled out an earphone, and smiled. "Can I help you gentlemen?"

The biggest one stepped forward. "You're one of Jax's mates, yeah? St. Edmund's?"

"And you are…?"

"We play your mate next week."

Jimmy raised an eyebrow. "Cool story, mate."

The third one chimed in. "Charlotte's looking good these days. Didn't peg her for the charity type."

That was it. Jimmy's grin faded, fists clenched. But he didn't swing first.

By the time word got to Jax, it was already too late. A Year Ten kid skidded to a halt in front of him, wide-eyed. "Jimmy got jumped. Three on one. Said something about Charlotte. About you."

Jax didn't wait. He just ran, faster than the wind could carry him. He found them behind the back sheds at St. Edmund's. Jimmy sat on the ground with a busted lip, blood on his school shirt, and one eye already swelling shut. Macca and Tino stood guard over him like sentries, tight-jawed, ready for round two if it came.

Jax dropped to one knee beside Jimmy. "What happened?"

Jimmy tried to shrug but winced from the effort. "Guess I finally said something they didn't like." And Jax saw that stubborn little half-smile Jimmy wore even with blood on his teeth.

It made him think of Charlotte's words: "You're not the only one who's learned to smile when it burns."

That night, Jax didn't go home straight away. He wandered through town, head down, fists jammed in his pockets, rage curled deep in his stomach. The old Jax would've found those Grammar boys and handled it. But not now; now he waited. He watched some film, trained harder, and when Saturday came, he laced up his boots like a soldier strapping in for war.

They thought they'd won by swinging fists in the shadows, but Jax knew where real battles were fought. Under lights, in front of a crowd, where scoreboards didn't lie.

# CHAPTER THIRTY-FOUR

Calm Before the Storm

The night before the game was still, unnervingly still. The kind of quiet that came just before the first crack of thunder. Jax lay in his bed, wide awake. The ceiling above blurred in and out of focus as flashes from his past flickered in his mind like faulty fluorescent lights.

He saw Jimmy on the ground, shirt ripped, blood dripping from his cut lip. Three-on-one, those bloody cowards. Jax hadn't been there to defend his mate, and that failure cut deep. Because he knew that feeling.

Another image rose in his mind: his younger self, crouched behind the lounge, clutching his knees while the yelling turned to glass breaking and fists flying. His father's rage, wild and unpredictable, often turned on him. His mother's silence, heavy and helpless, offered no shield. Back then, no one had come running. No one had stood up for Jax.

But Jax always had Jimmy's back, and tomorrow,

he'd show them. Not with fists, not like his old man. He'd show them with footy, because tomorrow, they played Newcastle Grammar, and this time, Jax wouldn't miss the fight.

He woke before dawn, not restless but sharp, a quiet clarity running through him. It was the calm before the storm—only this time, Jax was the storm. His boots felt lighter, his breathing smooth, his body alive with focus. The nerves had burned away, leaving only clarity in their place. And when he stepped into the changeroom, it wasn't fury that drove him but justice, a quiet justice carried not in words but in what he was about to do.

The ref's whistle blew, and from kick-off, Jax tore across the field like a man possessed. Each run carried a message, each tackle a warning, each try a declaration of war. "You messed with my brother. You thought we were weak. Now you know."

By halftime, Newcastle Grammar looked rattled; by fulltime, they were finished. Jax strode off the field, head lifted, boots heavy with mud, blood drying on his cheek. He didn't need to gloat. The game had been his voice.

The sheds were quieter now, the kind of quiet that came after the storm. Most of the boys had already scattered, chasing the adrenaline high and the bus ride home, but Jax had stayed, sweat still slick on his skin, mud drying on his calves, jersey ripped at the shoulder. His chest rose and fell, steady now, like something inside him had finally found a place where it belonged to.

That's when Troy walked in and sat beside him. Two worn-out souls, coach and player, man and boy, both, somehow, in between. "You did good today, kid," Troy said. Jax nodded. "You played like a man." A pause. Then, softer: "But you looked like a boy when you heard that Jimmy got hit."

Jax's head snapped toward him. "You saw?"

Troy nodded slowly. "From a distance. I was just coming out of a meeting when it was already over. Saw you standing there with him after."

Jax's throat tightened. "Why didn't you stop it?"

Troy sighed. "Because by the time I got there, it was done. All I could do was watch what came after. And what I saw… was you not backing away. That mattered."

Jax glanced at his muddied hands. Once, they'd curled into fists; now, they gripped footies, passed to teammates, lifted others up. "I wanted to kill them," he said, voice raw and angry.

"I know," Troy replied. "You could've."

"I still want to."

"But you didn't," Troy said, resting a hand on his shoulder. "You played them instead. You buried them where it counted." There was something in Troy's eyes, the same recognition Charlotte had written about in her letter, that he didn't always have to be the fire. But if he was… he could choose how to burn.

"Your old man's name follows you, but you're not him," Troy said. "That fire in you doesn't have to burn you up. It can drive you, if you let it. And today, you showed me which way you're leaning." The words stuck. "Proud of you, mate," Troy finished. "Bloody proud." Then he stood, patted Jax's back once, and left.

For a long moment, Jax just sat there, breathing, feeling that fire in his chest. Only now, it wasn't wild or angry, it was a controlled sort of calm, the kind he could finally carry.

# CHAPTER THIRTY-FIVE

## The Space Between

Charlotte's voice came from the doorway. "Didn't think you'd still be here." Jax looked up. She was leaning on the frame, hair pulled back, hands shoved in her jacket pockets. There was no crowd noise now, no buzz of voices, just the faint echo of a few boots on concrete as the last stragglers left.

He stood, running a hand over the back of his neck. "Didn't think you'd make it."

"I almost didn't," she said. Her voice was light, but her eyes weren't. "Congrats, though. You were… intense out there."

"That's the point," he laughed, trying to read her. "What's up? Something happen?"

She glanced past him, toward the empty benches. "Nothing. Just… you play like you're fighting ghosts."

"Maybe I am."

For a second, he thought she might press him, the

way she usually did. Instead, she stepped back. "Anyway, I've gotta go. My dad's waiting."

"That's it?" Jax asked. The question slipped out sharper than he meant.

"What do you want me to say, Jax?" She finally met his eyes, and there was something there, a weight he didn't understand. "You don't let anyone in unless it's on your terms. That's exhausting, sometimes."

Before he could answer, she was already walking out of the shed heading toward the car park, hands shoved deep into her jacket pockets.

Jax watched her go, the echo of her words settling in heavier than the win. He didn't know what he'd done wrong, only that the space between them suddenly felt wider than the field he'd just played on.

# CHAPTER THIRTY-SIX

The Turning Point

**W**alking through the school gates that day felt different. Not just for Jax but for everyone. For once, no one just looked *at* him; they looked *up* to him. A nod here, a shoulder pat there. Even the Year Twelve boys who used to sneer at him gave him space.

But the lift in the air didn't stop the words from ringing in his head. "You don't let anyone in."

Charlotte found him at recess, hair pulled into a no-nonsense tie, blazer crisp, the sleeves pressed into neat lines. She didn't bother to saying hello, skipping straight past small talk to ask "Why didn't you fight them?"

Jax shrugged. "I didn't need to. I just played them on the field instead."

She studied him for a moment, and he knew this was the point, the one where he could keep the walls up or let a crack show. "You were right," he said quietly. "I don't let people in because, I'm scared they'll leave. And if they do, I'm not sure I could take it again."

Her expression softened, her guard lowering just a fraction. "Jax, if you never let anyone in, you'll end up alone. Sometimes you've got to take the gamble. Vulnerability's not weakness, it's proof you care enough to risk getting hurt. And yeah, you might get wounded, but you might also find something that lasts, something worth it."

He just nodded, feeling the truth of her words sink in.

"I liked it better that way," she said. "You didn't look angry out there. You looked controlled and powerful."

Jax felt his ears go warm. "Thanks."

She leaned in just enough for him to hear. "It made me proud."And with that, she walked away, leaving him lighter and more unsettled all at once, his heart hammering harder than it ever had on a field.

That afternoon, he got home before his mum. The house was quieter, but not the kind of quiet that pressed on his chest. The air felt lighter, carrying the faint scent of lemon cleaner instead of stale smoke. The kitchen bench was clear, dishes stacked neatly in the rack. Even the old fridge looked different, stocked and organised, like someone cared what was in it.

On the milk was a sticky note in his mum's looping handwriting: *Bought groceries today. Back soon. LUB14.*

When she got home, her hair was tied back, uniform neatly pressed and her face tired but bright. She saw him waiting at the kitchen table. "You're home early," she said.

"Wanted to see you."

"Everything okay?"

"Yeah… actually, I think it is."

For the first time in a long while, they sat down to dinner together. They didn't shout, and they didn't sit in heavy silence either. They simply shared the space, enjoying each other's presence.

She told him she was back on the roster, two shifts this week, maybe more next. Her voice wavered with nerves, but underneath it was a quiet resolve. She was willing, trying.

"I watched your game," she added. "Online. One of the nurses had a son playing."

Jax blinked. "You did?"

She nodded, eyes glossy. "You were incredible, Son."

"I was thinking of you. Of Jimmy. Of everything."

She reached across the table and held his hand. "You've given me strength, Jax," she whispered. "Now use yours. Go change your stars."

And just like that, something internal shifted. Everything wasn't perfect, but for the first time, it felt possible.

# CHAPTER THIRTY-SEVEN

## Morning Light

Tuesday morning came gently. For the first time in years, Jax woke to the smell of bacon and eggs drifting down the hallway. Instead of smoke or silence or the stale buzz of a TV, the room was filled with breakfast. A proper breakfast. He rubbed his eyes, still half-caught in the dream that life might be shifting. The house felt different, lived in. Laughter hadn't returned yet, but the shadows were thinning.

He stepped into the kitchen and stopped. His mum was at the stove, hair tied up, dressing gown clean, tea in one hand, spatula in the other. There was colour in her cheeks and a vibrance in her eyes.

"Morning, Son," she said, like it was nothing unusual.

"Morning."

"How'd you sleep?"

"Great. Yeah… great."

She smiled, —strong, steady, real, vibrant. "Sit. Eat. You've earned it."

They didn't talk much. They didn't need to, the clink of cutlery, the warmth of food, the quiet between them was finally a comfortable space. For the first time in a long time, Jax didn't feel like the world rested entirely on his shoulders. She was standing now on her own. And maybe, just maybe, he could go back to being a kid for a little while longer.

Then came the knock at the door. His mum raised an eyebrow. "You expecting anyone, Son?"

Jax shook his head. She opened the door, and there stood Charlotte, hair loose, bag in hand, eyes bright but cautious.

"Hi… I was just wondering if Jax was home," she said softly. "I meant to come by earlier… I just wanted to check in. After the game."

His mum smiled. "Oh, you must be Charlotte. Jax has mentioned you."

Charlotte blushed. "Sorry for dropping in."

"Well," his mum said, smirking, "he didn't say you were *this* pretty."

"Mum," Jax groaned, grinning despite himself.

"Come in. I've just made breakfast. Are you hungry?"

"I'd love some, Mrs. Page."

And just like that, the house was full in a new way, full of something that had been missing for a long time. Hope.

# CHAPTER THIRTY-EIGHT

When Two Worlds Collide

That night, Jax lay on his bed staring at the cracked ceiling, one arm behind his head, the other resting over his chest where the letter from Charlotte remained folded in his journal. The air was warm, but his thoughts were warmer, slower, less jagged than they used to be.

He replayed the moment over and over again, Charlotte standing in his kitchen, smiling at his mum like she belonged there. And somehow, she did. The same girl who saw through his armour, who challenged his sharp tongue and softened his edges, had just shared eggs and small talk with the woman who had raised him through storms. Two worlds that once felt galaxies apart, now sitting at the same table.It shouldn't have worked, but it did.

There was something surreal about it, like the walls he'd built between his past and present had quietly crumbled to dust while he wasn't looking. For years, Jax had carried different parts of himself like secret compartments: the kid who'd been hurt, the teenager trying to rise, the boy who wrote poetry when no one was watching. But Charlotte hadn't just seen all those parts, she'd walked into them without fear.

And his mum didn't put on a mask, she didn't flinch or retreat, she welcomed Charlotte with a warmth he hadn't seen in years.

Maybe the life he'd always dreamed of wasn't something far off; maybe it had already started, in that kitchen, over eggs and half-smiles and a casual "You must be Charlotte." That moment, brief and domestic and ordinary as it was, felt like the most extraordinary thing he'd ever known. Two worlds had collided, and instead of breaking him, they made him whole.

Later that night, Jax scribbled a poem into his notebook, the kind he only wrote when his mind was full and his chest too tight to sleep.

When Two Worlds Collide
*I never thought she'd meet my mum.*
*Two parts of me I kept apart —*
*One full of storms, one full of light.*
*But they smiled like they'd known each other forever.*
*Maybe I don't have to split myself in two anymore.*
*Maybe I'm allowed to be whole.*

# CHAPTER THIRTY-NINE

Ghosts from the Past

The session had run long than expected, tackle drills, run through their plays, and edge defence. Coach Troy had them locked in, the way you did when you knew a season could make or break you.

Jax was last off the field, boots caked in dirt and grass, shoulders aching, but his mind strangely clear. He was halfway to the sheds, already picturing a long shower and dinner with his mum, when he noticed someone by the fence in faded jeans, hi vis work shirt, and sunnies perched on the brim of a dusty cap. He looked like he'd wandered in from another decade.

"Hey, mate," the man called. Jax slowed cautiously. "Oi, Jax. Hello. It's… it's your dad." He said it like he was expecting a big, warm hug, but that was the farthest thing in Jax's mind.

Jax's stomach tightened. "What are you doing here?"

"Oh, mate, I was just in the area. Heard a bit of buzz

about you lately, Newcastle's prodigy, huh?" The man grinned. "Couldn't believe it. I had to see it with my own eyes."

Jax didn't answer. Towel over one shoulder, boots in hand, he just stood there, staring through the man.

"You've made something of yourself," his dad went on. "Always knew you had fire in you. Glad you've learned to harness it."

Nothing from Jax. Just stillness.

"Anyway," his dad shrugged, "thought maybe we could grab a bite to eat at the old pub. My shout, of course."

"Nah," Jax said. "I'm heading home. Mum, Charlotte, and I have dinner plans."

"Oh…" His dad glanced away, then back. "How is she… your mum that is?"

"She's good," Jax said. "Back working. Clean. Stronger. Happier." He paused, eyes narrowing. "She did it without you. I did too."

His dad's smile faltered. "Yeah, well, you know how things were. They weren't easy for me either."

Jax looked at him, really looked. And for the first time, he didn't see a mystery or a monster or a missing piece. He just saw a man, ordinary and full of excuses. He didn't have anger or sadness, no aching for a father once lost. He realised he didn't need this man to apologise, or explain, or stay, or go. He didn't need him at all.

Because Jax had made it here without him. He'd picked up the pieces, carried his mum, rebuilt what had been broken, and now he was everything his father wasn't. The anchor in the storm, the one who stayed, and proof that blood didn't decide the man.

"I've gotta go," Jax said.

His dad nodded slowly. "Alright then. Maybe another time."

"Maybe."

But they both knew it wouldn't happen.

As Jax walked toward the sheds, twilight settling on the field, he felt something unfamiliar. Not glory or grudges; just freedom. For years, he'd believed he was damaged goods because his dad had left. But now, boots in one hand and towel in the other, he knew the truth. He'd been reforged. The fire inside him, once wild and dangerous, now burned steadily. For the first time, Jax didn't want it to torch the past. He wanted it to light the future, to change his stars.

# CHAPTER FORTY

## The Boy and the Flame

Later that week, Jax found himself back at the oval. It was empty and there were no whistles, no drills, no voices slicing through the air. The grandstand was bare, its seats catching the last light of day. The smell of cut grass lingered, mixing with the faint tang of liniment left over from the afternoon session.

He walked to the centre, the turf soft under his boots, and dropped the ball at his feet. It landed with a dull thud and stayed there, still as the air. He lowered himself to the grass, folding his legs, elbows resting loosely on his knees, and just breathed.

For the first time in what felt like forever, he felt still. There was no pressure bearing down on his chest, no storm clouds gathering in the corners of his mind, no fight-or-flight clawing under his skin. Just the steady inhale and exhale of someone who had walked through fire and come out forged, not burnt on the other side.

So much had changed. His mum was smiling again,

not that tight, rehearsed smile she used to wear like armour, but the unguarded kind that softened her whole face. Jimmy was laughing again, back to shit stirring in the best way possible. Charlotte was still there, sharp, kind, and fierce, the sort of girl who didn't just hold your hand but held the weight you carried without flinching.

And Troy was more than a coach now. A guide, a mirror, a mentor, proof that a man could be broken once and still be rebuilt. He wasn't Jax's father, but in every way that counted, he'd shown up like one.

Jax wasn't running anymore. Not from his past, not from his pain, not even from the idea of being happy. He wasn't out to prove himself to ghosts or reclaim what had been stolen. He was simply here, breathing and standing. His own man.

He lay back on the grass, eyes tracing the slow drift of clouds across the deepening sky. The floodlights clicked on somewhere in the distance, their hum a low reminder that night was coming. He thought about the boy who used to hide behind the couch, knees pressed tight to his chest, counting the seconds until the yelling stopped. About the kid who nearly gave up on himself because no one had shown him why he was worth saving.

And then he thought about the person here and now, calm, grounded, and steady, ready for what life had to offer.

He sat up and picked up the footy. It was scratched and scuffed, the grip worn smooth from years of use. But it still held its shape, still true, still strong. Just like him.

As the sun dipped behind the hill, the sky bled into deep orange and purple, a slow fade that made everything feel suspended in time. Jax smiled. He wasn't here to burn the world down anymore. He just wanted to light the way, steady, quiet, and sure.

Later that night, he opened his notebook and wrote.

*September 2nd.*

*Sat on the field tonight after training. No one around. Just me and the sky.*

*Didn't feel broken. Didn't feel angry. Felt like I was finally okay. Not perfect. But real.*

*I like this version of me. No masks. No hiding. Just here. Just enough. Just me.*

# CHAPTER FORTY-ONE

## The Ghosts Come for a Visit

Troy sat at the back of the Newcastle Knights meeting room, shoulders drawn in, cap brim low, trying to disappear into the shadows. He'd told himself it was just another building, just another club. But it wasn't.

The place was crowded—staff in polos, junior coaches with clipboards, scouts murmuring in the corners. Up front, the head coach ran the session, clicking through a projector of player footage: first-grade breakdowns, set-piece reviews, the all-too-familiar rhythm of a Monday morning session.

Troy kept his eyes down, but every detail dragged him backward. The last time he'd walked into this room he was twenty-four, limping on a ruptured ACL, numbed on painkillers, riding ego and vices he thought he could outrun. That one-year deal with the Knights had been his lifeline, his last chance to prove he wasn't the headline people whispered about.

But it ended the way they all predicted. He skipped rehab, turned up half-cut, lied about being clean, even bet on his own team.

The walls looked the same—framed jerseys, faded team photos, sweat ground into the carpet—but he wasn't. Or at least, he hoped he wasn't.

On the projector, the head coach flicked to Jax. Crashing into tackles. Barking orders. Dragging teammates with sheer will. Troy recognised that fire. He'd carried it once, but his own had burned reckless, untamed. Jax's was different, focused, aimed higher.

From across the room, a pair of eyes found him. Older now, lined, but unmistakable: an assistant coach who'd once fought for him. The man didn't smile or frown, just studied him with a look balanced between memory and caution.

When the meeting wrapped, chairs scraped back. The assistant walked over, arms folded.

"Didn't think we'd see you again," he said, voice flat but not unkind.

Troy nodded. "Didn't think I'd ever want to come back."

"You here for Jax?"

"Yeah."

Silence stretched, heavy with what neither said.

"You've done good with that kid," the assistant finally told him. "Whatever you're doing, keep it up. He's got something."

It wasn't applause, but it carried deeper. Something inside Troy eased—not pride yet, but close.

The head coach looked back over his shoulder. "You mentoring him?"

Troy nodded. "Trying to."

"Good," the coach said. "He listens to you. It shows."

Troy stayed quiet, letting the words settle in places he thought were burned out long ago.

When he finally stepped outside, the late light caught the dust in the air, turning the car park gold. The building behind him still held ghosts—the mistakes, the could-have-beens, the wasted nights. But they weren't chasing him anymore. Maybe he'd finally started to outrun them.

For the first time in years, Troy didn't walk away with shame in his gut.He walked away lighter. With hope.

# CHAPTER FORTY-TWO

## The Boy Who Stood Up

The plaza pulsed with weekend noise, buskers strumming by the fountain, kids spilling out of the cinema in noisy clusters, the smell of fried food hanging in the warm air. Jax walked alongside Charlotte, a Coke slushie in one hand, her fingers intertwined with his in the other. The day felt easy, almost boring. In his life, boring was a rare commodity.

Then he saw it. Up ahead, by the bins near the benches, three older boys in Meriwether State School uniforms had Matt Easton surrounded. They stood too close, moving like a pack that knew the scent of blood. One shoved him in the shoulder. Matt fumbled his drink, the lid popping off, liquid splattering down his shirt.

"Oi," the kid sneered. "What's the matter, princess? Forgot how to use your hands?"

Another stepped in, louder, sharper. "Do you guys at St. Edmund's wear skirts with your blazers?"

Laughter rang out from the three boys, the hollow, ugly kind. Matt stood still, shoulders squared but eyes low, his jaw clenched so tight it looked painful. He didn't offer a comeback or a fight, just silence, the kind that hung heavy between them.

Jax released Charlotte's hand and moved forward, calm and deliberate, steady as the tide drawing back from shore. "All right, boys," he said, voice calm but cut with enough steel to slice through their noise. "That's enough."

The tallest one turned mid-smirk, then froze. Recognition hit him like a slap across the face. "Relax, mate," he said, taking a half-step back. "We're just mucking around, Jax."

Jax didn't break stride. He stopped close enough that the kid had to tilt his chin to meet his eyes. His gaze was steady, heavy, and measured, the kind of look that carried weight without a fist behind it.

"Doesn't look like fun to me," Jax said.

The group's confidence cracked. One of them muttered, "Let's go," nudging the tall one. Their feet shifted, their shoulders folded in, and they broke apart, peeling back into the crowd, their bravado evaporating.

Matt let out a slow breath and hitched his bag higher on his shoulder, face blank like the whole thing had rolled off him. "Didn't need help," he muttered.

Jax gave a small nod. "Didn't say you did. Just don't let clowns like that rent space in your head. I wear the same colours as you, now. That makes us family."

Matt hesitated, then gave the smallest of nods. "Thanks."

Jax was about to walk back to Charlotte when Matt called after him. "Hey, we've got King's College next week. It's the final game."

"Yeah," Jax said. "Big one. Independent Catholic Colleges Cup."

Matt's lips twitched into a dry, knowing smile. "Been twenty-five years since we've won it. We need to be switched on to have any chance with them."

Jax's voice was quiet but certain. "Then let's make sure we are."

The tension, the rivalry, the grudges, they were all gone. It was just two players walking into the same fight, ready to lace up and chase something bigger than both of them.

# CHAPTER FORTY-THREE

The Final Game

The morning of the King's College game rolled in heavy and grey, the kind of coastal day where the clouds hung low and the breeze carried a salty bite. It wasn't raining, but the air felt charged, like the sky was holding its breath.

King's weren't just another opponent. They were a Sydney juggernaut, an old-money private school that turned out footy teams like factories turned out steel—polished, ruthless, and built to last. In the Independent Catholic Colleges Cup, they'd been untouchable for twenty-five years. They looked carved from stone, maroon and black jerseys stretched over broad chests, boots polished to a mirror shine, haircuts sharp enough to cut paper. This wasn't a team that rebuilt. They didn't need to. When one player fell, the next was already waiting, trained and hungry, as if the school itself kept producing them on an assembly line. Rugby league wasn't just played here; it was taught, studied, lived. Every year they arrived with the same swagger and precision, a private school army ready for war.

Beating them would be more than a win. It would be rewriting history.

Jax sat on the wooden bench in the sheds, taping his wrists slowly and deliberately while a trainer strapped his ankles. His boots sat neatly beside him, laces open like waiting hands. Around him, the boys moved in their own pre-game rhythms—some rolling out tight muscles, others stretching, a few pacing the floor like caged animals. A portable speaker rattled the walls, the bassline hammering in Jax's chest.

Troy's voice cut through the noise. "Specs."

Jax looked up. The coach stood at the doorway, cap low, eyes steady. He beckoned Jax over, lowering his voice once he was close.

"They're here," he said, nodding towards the sideline.

Jax followed his gaze through the open tunnel. A small knot of men in red and navy polos stood watching the warm-ups, clipboards in hand, radios crackling, sharp eyes taking everything in.

"Knights scouts," Troy said.

"I see 'em," Jax replied quietly.

"You don't have to be perfect today," Troy told him. "Just present. Back yourself."

The whistle shrieked and the game cracked open like thunder. From the first carry, King's flew up in a blur of maroon and black, their line speed ferocious. Tackles landed with a jolt you felt in your teeth—

shoulders colliding, bodies smacking the turf, breath ripped from lungs. Every pass from their halves was crisp, every set rolled forward like it had been scripted days before. They weren't just playing footy, they were running a blueprint, every movement rehearsed and ruthless.

St. Edmund's fought to hang on, but the tide never turned. Each set pushed them deeper, each kick forced them back into their own red zone. By halftime, the scoreboard glared eighteen to nil. Battered, bruised, and pinned in their own half, the boys looked less like a team chasing history and more like survivors waiting for rescue.

## Halftime

The sheds smelled of sweat, liniment, and damp jerseys. Boys slumped on benches, breathing hard, heads down. Some stared at the floor, others at the scoreboard in their heads.

Jax sat with his elbows on his knees, sweat dripping from his jaw. A thin trickle of blood snaked from the cut above his eyebrow, marking his face like war paint. His chest heaved, but his eyes were sharp.

Troy paced in front of them. "Eighteen points. That's all. We get the next one and we're back in it."

Someone muttered about the size of King's pack. Another about their pace.

"Doesn't matter," Jax said suddenly, cutting through the murmurs. His voice wasn't loud, but it carried. "We've trained for this. We know who we are. We've come back before, and we can do it again. They're not better than us. They're just winning."

The boys lifted their heads.

"Next forty minutes," Jax went on. "That's all that matters. No regrets. Leave it all out there on the field."

## Second Half

From the moment they ran back out, St. Edmund's looked different, spring in their step.

Jax started demanding the ball, darting in and away on the edge, hammering into tackles, barking the lift call to drive his teammates off the defensive line. One line-break down the sideline and he was over in the corner for the first try. Minutes later, he set up another with a slick face-ball inside, cutting the defence wide open.

Then came Matt's moment. A gap opened, Matt punched through, and with a brilliant offload found Jax, who flicked it quickly to the fullback supporting inside. Try. Suddenly it was eighteen to twelve. The crowd roared.

St. Edmund's pressed again. Another wide ball found Jax, who burned his man by stepping inside then out, before diving over in the corner. Eighteen all. The conversion missed, but the game was alive.

King's hit back with raw power, pounding through the middle before swinging the ball wide. Their winger dived over in the corner. The kicker lined up the conversion, but the breeze carried it left of the uprights. No goal. The score stayed at twenty-two to eighteen, with only two minutes left on the clock.

## The Call

Huddled under their own posts, St. Edmund's sucked in oxygen like lifeblood. Sweat dripped, lungs heaved, but eyes stayed locked on Jax.

"This is it," he said, voice firm. "Short kick-off, my side. Trust me."

The kicker nodded. The huddle broke, boys jogging into position, nerves stretched tight as wire. The referee's whistle cut the air. The kicker steadied, breathed once, then drove through the ball. *Bang.* It climbed high, tumbling end over end toward the sideline.

Jax sprinted, eyes fixed, timing his run. He launched into the contest, twisting midair, arms outstretched. For a heartbeat, it was him against the pack, bodies colliding, hands clawing upward, and then the ball was his. He ripped it down like he'd stolen it from the gods. The crowd erupted.

St. Edmund's surged forward, hit-up after hit-up, patient but urgent. The ball shifted edge to edge, testing the defence, looking for a crack. Then Jax saw it. He raised his arm and barked, "Boss! Boss!"

It was an override call, rarely used. It meant he'd spotted something; a tired defender, an overlap, a gap where there shouldn't have been one. His teammates knew the signal. They adjusted their lines. The play was on.

The halfback snapped the ball wide, flat and fast. Jax angled his run perfectly, slicing between two defenders like a blade through paper. He burst clear, diving low as arms clawed at him, and grounded the Steeden over the line. Try. The scoreboard lit: twenty-two all. Kick to come.

## The Kick

He turned to the kicker, steadying him with a hand on the shoulder. "Take your time. You've got this. I believe in you."

Ten seconds left. The crowd hushed, a silence heavy enough to feel in the chest. The kicker stepped back, drew in a long breath, held it, then struck with military precision.

For an instant, everything slowed. Jax's gaze flicked to the stands, where Tino was already grinning, like he'd run the numbers before the ball even left the boot. The ball sailed high, straight and true, splitting the uprights clean between the black dot.

Twenty-four to twenty-two.

The whistle blew.

The sideline erupted. Boys piled into each other, shouting, laughing, crying, the weight of twenty-five years finally breaking loose. In the chaos, Jax swore he heard Charlotte's voice rise above the din, calling his name.

## The Aftermath

Later, in the sheds, steam curled through the air, mixing with sweat, mud, and the sting of liniment. The boys slumped on benches, spent, voices hoarse from victory.

Troy appeared out of the haze with a Knights assistant at his shoulder. "He's ready," the assistant said.

Troy turned to Jax. "They want you in at the club for a meeting."

Jax didn't answer straight away. He sat there, boots loose, jersey clinging to his skin, feeling the weight of it—everything he'd been, everything he'd carried, everything still ahead.And when he finally rose, slinging his boots over his shoulder and stepping out into the night air, it didn't feel like a dream.

It felt like destiny.

# CHAPTER FORTY-FOUR

Changing His Stars

Jax walked out of the McDonald Jones Stadium with a contract folder tucked under one arm and a grin that stretched ear to ear, thinking about everything he'd crawled through to get here.

A ten-year deal. *Top 30*. It was not a whisper anymore, a maybe. The *Top 30* was the club's main squad, the thirty best players in the club signed to full-time NRL contracts. They were the ones eligible to run out in first grade every weekend.

No more development lists, no more training and trials. It meant he was in, one of them. And he'd earned every inch of it.

His old pickup idled in the car park, windows down, engine humming. Nothing flashy—just Troy's battered ute, passed down to him as a final gift. It wasn't bright or shiny, but it had seen its scars, worn its dents, carried its weight. Rugged. Earned. A vehicle built for hard yards, not glamour. Which made it perfect. In the passenger seat, Charlotte sat in sunnies, her smile quiet and certain. In the back, Macca, Tino, and Jimmy were wrestling over who got to pick the playlist while shouting about where they were going for dinner.

"Come on, Mr. Superstar!" Macca yelled. "Get in before Jimmy eats all the bloody snacks!"

Jax opened the door. Before he could even sit down, Jimmy leaned forward with a grin that was all teeth and mischief. "Ten-year deal? Surely there's room in the squad for a team comedian?"

Tino nodded, mock-serious. "Or a strategy coach. I've been perfecting my theories on kicking angles and wind resistance."

Macca slapped him on the shoulder. "You better be shouting dinner, ya tight bastard."

Jax laughed, the deep belly kind, the kind that sat in your chest and reminded you that you were alive. These were his people. His crew. Charlotte reached over and squeezed his hand. "I'm proud of you," she said, soft and low.

His phone buzzed in his pocket. He pulled it out.

*[Mum]: Proud of you, baby boy. LUB14.*

He stared at the message for a moment, heart catching in his throat. LUB14, love you always. Something only they knew. A language born from hard days and quiet hope.

He slid the phone back in his pocket and shifted the ute into gear. As they rolled through town, past his old school, the takeaway place where they used to hang out, and the pub that once haunted him but also held his turning point, Jax no longer felt the weight of the past. He felt fire, the kind you carried and mastered, the kind that lit the way forward.

He wasn't the boy under table six any longer or the angry kid staring out the window, waiting for a father who never came, or the kid with too many secrets and nowhere to put them. He was not a boy, but a man who carried the fire now.

They drove on, boots in the tray, mates' laughter spilling out the back, Charlotte's hand warm in his. Jax didn't look back. He knew now he could go anywhere, take anything life threw at him, and flip it from wreckage to gold. Because the stars weren't something you were born under, they were something you could reach for and claim.

# CHAPTER FORTY-FIVE

## The Last Page

The lights from the McDonald Jones Stadium bled into the night sky, a soft halo over the town that had built Jax, broken him, and somehow put him back together.

The stands were empty now. The roar of the thirty-five-thousand-strong crowd had faded to a memory, replaced by the low hum of the floodlights and the soft sea breeze drifting in from the coast. Jax had walked up from the sheds alone, boots unlaced, jersey clinging to his back, still heavy with sweat. His body ached in that good way that told you every hit, every run, every scrap of breath had been worth it. In the back of his throat, he could taste the faint tang of blood, the kind you only got after a real contest.

Tonight had been his first game as a professional. Eighteen years old, and he'd run out under those lights wearing the blue and red colours of the Newcastle Knights for real.

He sat halfway up the stand, eyes fixed on the empty field, the dead patches near the posts, the divots ripped through the middle, the sideline where he'd flown, the ground he'd bled for, the ground he'd owned. He pulled his kit bag onto his lap, running a thumb over the Knights logo stitched into the fabric. The dream wasn't a dream anymore. It was his.

His mind drifted back to a sticky floor in an old Newcastle pub, a table too big for a boy to hide beneath, and a screen above him blazing with footy. He remembered thinking: One day, that'll be me. One day, they'll be screaming my name.

And here he was. Not the lost kid waiting by the window, not the teenager smiling through smoke, not the boy scribbling poems in secret. Tonight, he wasn't fragments of the past. He was all of them at once, standing whole, ready for what came next.

Jax stood, slung the bag over his shoulder, and took one last look at the field.

He wasn't the boy under the table anymore, staring up at a world that didn't see him. He was the man at his own table now, and every chair beside him was fought for and never handed over.

He fixed his eyes on the path ahead and walked it head-on, carried by no fear, no doubt, only the unshakable clarity of who he had become.

# EPILOGUE

## Let It Burn

Troy stood on the sideline of a dusty training oval, clipboard in hand, whistle hanging loose around his neck. The air smelled faintly of cut grass and boot leather. Beyond the fence, cicadas hummed in the fading heat. The sun was dipping low, spilling gold across the grass, and the late-afternoon stillness carried that quiet magic that only came after hours of hard work.

Out on the field, a pack of teenagers jogged the last lap of training. They moved in a clump, one tripping over another's boot, two laughing so hard they nearly collapsed, but still pushing forward together. A team. And in every grin, every shove, every lung-burning step, Troy saw it—the same hunger, the same spark.

He thought of Jax. Jax, who had become everything Troy had once prayed the boy could be—strong, grounded, fearless, and full of a heart that kept giving. A kid who had taken pain and forged it into purpose.

Troy remembered the first time he'd seen him, with his quiet, angry eyes, the guarded way he carried himself, the way he'd almost dared the world to underestimate him. But even then, there had been something else. A flicker, a small light that refused to go out.

He'd worried every day that Jax might take the wrong turn, the one Troy had taken himself, down roads lined with regret and bad choices. But Jax had carved his own path, and in doing so, he'd shown Troy there was still time to carve out his own.

Troy raised the whistle to his lips and blew, the sharp blast dragging him out of his thoughts. The boys groaned as he called for one more set of sprints. "Come on!" he yelled. "You've got more in you than that. Earn it!"

They ran, arms pumping, legs burning, breath ragged. And Troy felt something in his chest loosen, the way it did when you knew you were exactly where you were meant to be. He wasn't just a washed-up footy player anymore. He was a mentor, a guide. A man who was still healing but no longer running from the shadows of his past.

When the last lap ended, the boys collapsed in the grass, laughing between gulps of air. One of them, the smallest in the squad, gave him a cheeky grin and called out, "That all you got for us, Coach?"

Troy chuckled. "Not even close, mate. You lot are just getting started."

He looked down at the clipboard, then back to the group. They were tired, sweaty, and grinning like idiots, and they had no idea how much potential they carried.

Troy smiled. Because the fire that had once burned him was now the fire lighting the way for the next generation. The fire was theirs now, to light their way. As the boys gathered their gear, Troy's phone buzzed in his pocket. He pulled it out. He had one new message, from Jax, and it read: "LUB14." Just the code. He didn't need the rest.

Troy slipped the phone away, glanced once more at the fading sun, and blew his whistle. The sound cut sharp through the hum of cicadas, calling the boys back in.

The fire kept burning, and it would keep burning, in them and in him, a beacon for the lost, a weapon for the willing, a light that would outlast the shadows.

# AUTHOR'S NOTE

I wrote *The Boy Who Played With Fire* for every kid who's ever felt like they weren't enough, for every teen who's carried more than they should, for anyone who's been told they're unlovable, unworthy, too angry, too soft, or too different for this world.

I've been that kid. I've walked through storms without a map or compass. I've found my way by instinct, grit, and by leaning on the good people who refused to give up on me.

Jax isn't just a character, he's a reflection of thousands of boys I've worked with and coached. Misunderstood, full of potential, burning with questions no one ever helped them answer. A mix of toughness and tenderness we rarely see on the surface, but that lives in so many hearts. He's proof that you can come from pain and still build purpose, that you can take what tried to break you and turn it into something that makes you stronger.

If you've struggled with identity, grief, rage, shame,

or hopelessness, if you've ever felt invisible, I hope you found a part of yourself in these pages. Your story isn't over. Keep going.

Remember this: fire doesn't always destroy. In the right hands, it can forge strength instead of ruin. It can give warmth instead of burning you. When understood and harnessed, fire becomes more than a force—it becomes fuel. A light. A way forward.

Lead with kindness, stay resilient, and chase your dreams. And if someone out there is your reason to keep going, never let them doubt it.

— Liam Mulhall